FOREVER MINE

THE MURPHY CLAN—RETURN TO HOPE'S CROSSING

KATHY COATNEY

Windtree
Press

COPYRIGHT

ACKNOWLEDGMENTS

My faithful email check-in pals, Jennifer Skullestad and Lisa Sorensen; my critique partner, Luann Erickson; my beta reader, Rebecca Clark— you are my GPS to finding the end.

Friends and family made the journey memorable—Susan Crosby, Karol Black, Georgia Bockoven, Diana McCollum, Tammy Lambeth, Libby Hall, Shari Boullion, Diana Robertson, Terry McLaughlin, and Patti Berg, and my family—Nick, Wade and Devin and Collin, Jake and Emily and Allie and Russell. I'm blessed to have had you all beside me.

I've also had the pleasure to work with several talented business-women: Laura Shin, my editor, TINB Ink, and Tara with Fantasia Frog Design, my cover designer.

ALSO BY KATHY COATNEY

Thank you for reading *Forever Mine,* the second book in the *Return to Hope's Crossing* series, part of *The Murphy Clan*. *The Murphy Clan* can be read as stand alone books, but there are also three series within the Clan— *Return to Hope's Crossing*, *Falling in Love*, and the *Crooked Halo Christmas Chronicles*. Book two, *Forever Yours*, Willa and Ben's story will be out March 2021.

If you liked this book, please leave a review. It is the best way to thank an author for a memorable read.

I love hearing from my fans. You can contact me through my website, newsletter, or join my Facebook group Kathy Coatney's The Beauty Bowl. I share information about my books, excerpts, and other fun information. If you like free books come join Kathy Coatney's Review Team by sending me an email kathy@kathycoatney.com.

All my books are small town, contemporary romances with uplifting stories of hope, a sprinkling of quirky characters and a happily ever after.

Contact me at:

Website

Kathy Coatney's The Beauty Bowl

The Murphy Clan

Return to Hope's Crossing series

Forever His

Forever Mine

Forever Yours

Falling in Love series

Falling For You...Again

Falling in Love With You

Falling in Love For The First Time

Crooked Halo Christmas Chronicles

Be My Santa Tonight

Her Christmas Wish

Under the Mistletoe

Crooked Halo Christmas Chronicles Boxset

Other Contemporary Romances

Leave Me Breathless

A Romantic Mystery

FOREVER MINE

He's lost everything that gave his life meaning. She's determined to show him that she's his new beginning.

Cassie Cooper's neat, orderly life is turned topsy-turvy when overnight she becomes a single mom to three rambunctious boys. Between running her beauty salon and caring for her new charges, she has no time for a relationship. But love is definitely in the air when her childhood friend, Griffin Valentine, moves back to town.

Griffin Valentine, famed orthopedic surgeon, walks away from a lucrative practice after his two-year-old son dies in a car accident and his wife divorces him. Returning to Hope's Crossing to take over a small medical practice, he throws himself into caring for his patients. As much as he's drawn to Cassie and her readymade family, the past looms over him, threatening to destroy the new life he's building.

Can Cassie help Griffin find the courage to love again? Get your copy today because a second change at love doesn't come along every day!

Hope's Crossing, Indiana

The McDonald sisters sat under hair dryers and gossiped, their shouting so loud it muted the bowling balls hitting the pins in the bowling alley on the other side of the glass wall.

Cassie Cooper, owner of Sittin' Pretty, the beauty salon inside her Great-Aunt Luella's Beauty Bowl—bowling alley, restaurant, and community center—stared into the open desk drawer at a pair of foam earplugs. She closed the drawer and the temptation to use them. While the two sisters could drive her crazy at times, she loved them dearly.

Eleanor's shout drew her attention back to her clients. "Matilda, did you hear that Charlie Perkins's dog is expecting another litter of puppies?"

"Charlotte Peterman is pregnant? For heaven's sakes, she collects Social Security," Matilda shouted back.

"No, I said Charlie Perkins."

"Charlie's pregnant. How is that possible?"

"No, I said, Charlie's dog is."

Cassie pressed her lips together to suppress a laugh, blotting the perspiration dotting her forehead. Then again not all information was news worthy.

She crossed over and inched down the thermostat and felt a rush of cool air.

The timer dinged. She took Matilda out from under the dryer and commenced to comb out her short, wiry, gunstock-gray hair.

Without Eleanor to shout at, Matilda turned her attention to Cassie. "Did you hear that Griffin Valentine bought the place down the road from you?"

Cassie made an appropriate noise to indicate she was listening, but didn't comment beyond that. Matilda's raised brows told her she was fishing for information, and Cassie wasn't about to oblige her. If the local gossipmonger wanted to know more, she'd have to look elsewhere.

Griffin, Sam, and Emma had protected her from speculation every time her mother left her with Aunt Luella and Uncle Albert. Now it was her turn to shield Griffin from the small town busybodies. But more than that she didn't want to discuss Griffin or her reaction to him now that he'd returned to Hope's Crossing.

A joyous shout drew Cassie's attention to the bowling alley as her youngest charge, nine-year-old Jeff, high-fived Kevin Parker, her cousin Emma's son. Jeff's brothers, were on the next lane with two of their friends, and for once, the two weren't tormenting their younger brother.

It had been over a year since her cousin, Raymond, had dropped by to visit Aunt Luella, meaning hit her up for money. When she refused, he went out for a drink, and never returned, leaving the children behind. Since both of Raymond's parents were dead, Cassie had taken the kids in the same as Aunt Luella and Uncle Albert had done for her.

Cassie exhaled recalling her life BC—before children. She'd had a long list of rules not that long ago if she looked at the calendar, but now it felt like a lifetime ago. BC, she'd never left the house without her hair styled and makeup applied, and she'd never ever used a pony-tail or baseball cap to cover a bad hair day. BC, everything in its place and a place for everything, but the demands of parenting a nine, ten, and twelve-year-old had brought that to a screeching halt. These days her home had the remnants of a tornado passing through on an hourly basis.

Matilda quirked a snowy brow. "It would certainly be handy to have Griffin within calling distance with all the mischief those boys get into."

Cassie bristled. The boys were a handful no question, but she didn't appreciate the insinuation they were undisciplined. And to be fair, their behavior probably had more to do with her inexperience as a parent.

"My boys aren't troublemakers."

"Your boys? I thought they were Raymond's. Did you hear that, Eleanor? Cassie's taken custody of Raymond's boys."

"Cassie's making custard? Here?"

Matilda scowled at her sister. "She can't hear a blessed thing anymore."

Cassie swore under her breath. After a year, she'd come to think of them as hers, but she didn't want that bit of information all over town, especially since they were Raymond's children.

Picking up the curling iron, she did some finishing touches on Matilda's hair.

Matilda changed the subject. "Now that your cousin, Bella, is remarried and having a baby, that leaves you the only single one of the group."

"Yes'm, you're right, sister," Eleanor shouted.

Cassie sucked in a breath as Matilda's comment needled her like scissors to an open wound. Simultaneously thrilled and jealous for her cousins, they had what she'd always dreamed of—a big wedding with family and friends, a husband she loved, and children. So far Mister Right had been Mister Wrong. She wanted a man like her uncle—kind, caring and devoted to her Aunt Luella until the day he'd died and she refused to settle for anything less.

The timer dinged and Cassie blew out a sigh of relief as she shut off Eleanor's dryer. At least their shouting would drop a decibel.

Ha! The two continued to yell back and forth, which inspired Cassie to finish their comb-outs in record time.

Fifteen minutes later, she ushered the sisters out the door, then got the boys settled in the kitchen with their lunch. Realizing she'd forgotten her lunch at the salon, she went back to grab it, and the phone rang. She penciled in a color for Beatrice Wright—the sweetest lady in five counties. Cassie had yet to convince her that jet black wasn't the best choice for her coloring. She didn't have the heart to tell Beatrice it made her look like an eighty-year-old Elvira.

She'd barely hung up the phone when it rang again, this time with more appointments for homecoming—cuts, styles, and highlights. The event was still two months away, but everyone made their appointments early to ensure they looked their best for the big event. She could set the clock on an increase in business around the Hope's Crossing High School social calendar.

By the time she made it back to the kitchen, the boys had finished eating and her cousin, Emma, had arrived with her six-month-old daughter, Annie, in a front pack.

"Come on, boys. I want to get to the field before Annie falls asleep." Emma bounced the baby up and down to keep her from fussing.

Cassie had never seen the boys grab their gear as quickly for her as they did for Emma. "Thanks for picking them up. They've talked nonstop about going to play ball with Kevin at the ballpark."

"I should be the one thanking you. Kevin will have playmates while Sam and I go over the books and get ready for the playoffs."

The cowbell clanked as the boys shoved open the door and raced outside before Cassie could tell them goodbye, so instead she blew a raspberry on Annie's cheek that set off a peal of giggles. A pudgy hand swatted at her cheek. Cassie kissed it, and Annie clutched a fistful of her hair with the other hand.

"You little stinker." Cassie extricated the baby's fingers and took a step back to see her grinning devilishly.

"Approach at your own risk," Emma said between chuckles.

"Now you tell me."

"What would be the fun in forewarning you?"

Cassie laughed. "I'll pick them up after I close the shop."

"If we finish before you're done, we'll be at the house."

Cassie gave her cousin a hug and Annie another kiss, then watched them head out the door before going back to the salon for her one o'clock appointment.

She didn't get another break until four when she had a cancellation. She made herself a cup of coffee and sat down in the tiny office hidden away from the bowling alley. Propping her feet on the counter, she took out her phone scrolling through videos featuring hair braiding. She searched wedding hairstyles, looking for that perfect look her clients were always wanting—*and her*.

She pushed aside the pesky reminder of her single status and skimmed through social media until Joshua's picture filled the screen, his arm around a curvy brunette. She couldn't stop herself from clicking on the album. All their wedding photos came up, including several videos. She tapped on one and watched a beautiful fairytale wedding unfold. The first dance started and the band played *Love Me Forever*—the exact song she would have chosen.

Ten months after their breakup he'd married someone else. Resentment burned deep. They'd been together two years, and he'd never once hinted at marriage. Damn it, this should have been her friends and family celebrating her nuptials!

How could Joshua have left her when she'd needed him most?

CHILDISH LAUGHTER DREW Griffin Valentine away from his desk and the stack of files he'd spent his Saturday catching up on. Before he could move to the window his cell phone rang. He looked at the number and saw his mother calling him again.

As he crossed to the window, he answered the call, "Hey Mom. How's the cruise?"

"Wonderful."

She chattered on about all the ports of call she and Herb, the man she'd married after his father died, had visited. He'd never seen her happier than after she married Herb. They'd moved to Florida and were both retired now and traveled constantly.

Griffin stared out the window at the park across the street overflowing with parents and children. A toddler squealed in delight as his father scooped him up and swung him high in the air.

Memories rushed back. Once upon a time, he'd been that father out in the sweltering August heat playing with his son, Bobby.

Griffin stared at the framed photo of his son on the corner of his file cabinet beside him. He traced a finger over the metal frame where Bobby grinned back at him. Two years ago, he'd had a thriving practice as an orthopedic surgeon, a wife and son, then it all vanished on a snowy November day when a car accident took his son's life.

"Griffin, are you there?"

He blinked and pushed aside the past, compartmentalizing it just as his father had taught him. Becoming a physician, his father told him, meant controlling your emotions, and Griffin had learned from the best. "I'm here. Where are you now?"

"The Caribbean. Are you going to answer my question?"

Busted. "Sorry Mom, I spaced out."

"I asked if you were at home?"

"No, I'm at the office finishing up on some paperwork."

His mother made a tsking sound. "It's Saturday. Why aren't you outside enjoying the beautiful summer weather?"

"I was just about to head out when you called."

Silence.

"You know it's a sin to lie to your mother."

He winced. She knew him too well.

"Don't end up married to your career, Griffin. It's a lonely existence. Just look at your father for evidence of that."

It was true. His father had worked incessantly right until the heart attack that took him from them. And he and his brothers had followed in his footsteps. He rarely saw either of them because they were always working. Ben, a high school teacher in Chicago and Zeke, a trauma surgeon on another tour in Iraq.

Griffin had emulated his father's work ethic and paid a heavy price.

During his marriage Mary, his ex-wife, had continually accused him of hiding his feelings from her long before their son died. From the moment he'd rushed into the ER to find his son's lifeless body, he'd efficiently taken care of the funeral arrangements, contacting friends and family, comforting his wife, and accepting condolences, but he'd been frozen inside.

In the days following the funeral, he'd thrown himself into his work to avoid the silence at home. One night a few weeks after Bobby died, he'd come home from work, to find Mary's suitcases at the door. She'd said nothing, but the accusation in her eyes had spoken volumes. The instant the door closed behind her, he'd fallen apart.

"I know, Mom. I'm changing. I swear."

"Except that you're working on a Saturday. Are you dating anyone?"

Griffin swallowed a groan. "Not at the moment."

Another beat of silence that had him shifting from foot to foot like a recalcitrant child.

Her voice was a soft whisper of sound when she spoke. "I know it's hard to start over, but you have to. The saddest thing besides losing my grandson is seeing my son hurting and alone."

Griffin stared at Bobby's photo, recalling those first weeks and months when grief consumed his every waking moment. Then one day he woke up without remembering. A few weeks later, he'd treated a toddler and hadn't been paralyzed with memories of Bobby. Now, only a dull ache filled him when a memory caught him unaware. What if he stopped remembering Bobby altogether?

"You're on cruise control, Griffin. You function, you go through the day, but you're still numb inside."

He didn't deny his mother's statement, but she was wrong. The numbness had worn off long ago. All he knew was work. He might be a successful doctor, but he was a colossal failure at relationships. He stared out at the park filled with activity, then his silent, empty office. He couldn't deny there was nothing worse than being alone—*nothing*.

"Promise me you'll leave the office and go meet up with Sam and Emma. Drive to Chicago and see your brother, or better yet, take

Cassie out to dinner and a movie. I'm sure she could use a break from pandemonium of single parenting."

His mother repeatedly nudged him toward Cassie, but he'd resisted. They were friends—nothing more, but this time his Mom was right. What he needed was a little chaos in his life, and he knew exactly where to find it—Cassie.

In all the years he'd known Cassie, he'd never associated her with disorder—until Raymond's boys arrived. Then he'd gotten a glimpse of the unvarnished Cassie Cooper, and he liked her a lot.

"I'm walking out the door right now, so stop worrying about me and go enjoy yourself. You're on vacation."

He disconnected the call before she could comment. He grabbed his baseball cap from the hook by the door and went out to his truck. Minutes later, he pulled into the Beauty Bowl just before five. It was inconsiderate to show up at closing on a Saturday night for a haircut, but he headed inside determined to forge ahead with his plan to start living again.

The cowbell clanked as he pushed open the double glass doors. He waved to Donnie Baker working the counter, but no Luella. She was most likely in the kitchen at the grill.

He crossed the black and white checkered floor and headed for Sittin' Pretty. The lights were on, but no one was inside. He pushed open the door and called out Cassie's name.

Silence.

A sniffle—a Cassie sniffle. He'd know that sound anywhere. Dainty, neat, not the boisterous, over-the-top, dramatic sobbing, like Mary's had been. On the rare occasion he'd witnessed Cassie crying, it had eaten him up inside. Today was no different.

He hurried into the alcove to find tears streaming down her face as she stared at her phone. He squatted beside her and tucked a strand of silky blonde hair behind her ear. "What's wrong?"

She raised red-rimmed blue eyes. Eyes so huge and clear, they seemed to see right into his soul. She launched herself into his arms, her damp cheek pressed against his neck.

He tightened his arms around her, inhaling the sweet scent of her fancy salon shampoo and fresh country air. Delicate fingers squeezed his shoulders, and it occurred to him that she fit perfectly in his arms.

Cassie pressed her cheek tighter against his neck, then relaxed and pulled back. She swiped the tears from her cheeks, then averted her gaze. "It's nothing."

He studied her puffy eyes. "Doesn't look like nothing to me."

She shrugged off his comment. "You know me, I've always been overly sensitive."

Not true. She might appear soft and vulnerable on the outside, but she had an inner strength he'd always admired.

Griffin gently cupped her chin and tilted it until they were eye-to-eye. "That was more than a little cry."

Tears welled in her eyes again, and her anguish ate at him. "Maybe, but it's over now and I feel better."

"You know, I'm always available if you need to talk."

She nodded and swallowed, her eyes still damp and glistening. "Thanks, but I'm okay—really."

He didn't believe her, but he helped her to her feet and heard music coming from her phone as the video she'd been watching started playing. Her body tensed, and a tear slipped past her defenses. She quickly tapped the screen, and silence engulfed them.

She cleared her throat, and her voice came out bright and cheery as if she hadn't been crying seconds ago. "What are you doing here?"

Griffin wanted to press her about the video. Instead, he followed her cues. "I was hoping I could talk you into a haircut, but it can wait."

She glanced at the clock on the wall. "No, I can do it. I need to call Emma and let her know I'm going to be late picking up the boys."

Griffin debated telling her he didn't want to inconvenience her, but he couldn't bear the thought of going home to his empty, silent house. He'd much rather stay here with Cassie and find out what had upset her.

"Will you lock the door?" she asked as she tapped in Emma's number.

As he turned the lock, he heard her connect with Emma.

"Hey, Em, it's me. I'm going to be a little late picking up the boys."

He could faintly hear Emma's voice, volunteering to keep them overnight.

"Oh, that's too much," Cassie said. "I can't let you do that."

He heard Emma's voice turn indignant.

"Okay, I'm sorry. I know you're perfectly capable of taking care of all of them. Geez, you sound like Aunt Luella."

He couldn't hear Emma's response, but Cassie sounded hesitant. "Okay, I'll see you in the morning. Thanks."

Could it be she didn't want to be alone tonight any more than he did?

She tucked her phone into her back pocket and gestured to the salon chair. "Have a seat."

As soon as he was settled, she draped a towel over his shoulders and pinned it together at his throat, then snapped on a nylon cape. He followed her over to the sink, closed his eyes, and relaxed as those delicate fingers massaged his scalp, sending tingles along his spine and straight to his groin.

Before he knew it, she was leading him back to the salon chair.

"So, what are you going to do with a free evening on your hands?" he asked.

"Taking a long, hot bath!"

Her immediate response sent an image of steam, bubbles, and rosy pink skin to mind. A response stirred deep within him. He shifted to cover his reaction.

If Cassie noticed, she hid it well.

"How about before you do that, you join me for dinner at Little Italy?" Little Italy made the best pasta in town—actually the only pasta in town.

She froze, the scissors open and ready to snip as her baby blues met his in the mirror. "Are you asking me on a date?"

"I am," he said without hesitation.

Confusion marred her expression. "We've always been friends. Why would you want to date me all of the sudden, especially when you know my life is day-to-day chaos."

He snorted. "Compared to a silent, empty house, bedlam is the next best thing to heaven."

Her eyes widened and he saw pain there, but instead of grieving for herself, Griffin knew she was thinking of him and what he'd lost.

"Stop that!"

She dropped the scissors, and they clattered to the floor. "I'm, I'm sorry." She turned away and grabbed a new pair from the tray.

Griffin blew out a breath and touched her arm. "I'm sorry, Cass. I didn't mean to snap at you. I'm just tired of being the guy everyone feels sorry for. I just want to—"

When he didn't continue, the whisper of her voice tickled his ear. "Want to what?"

In the past he'd have changed the subject, but he gave her the unvarnished truth. "I just want to be a guy asking a girl I like to have dinner with me." He stared at her lips, so full and lush, begging for his touch, and for once he followed the urging of his heart and traced his fingertip over them. They were as soft and smooth as the finest silk.

She sighed. "Why did you do that?"

"Because I've wanted to do it for the longest time and now just seemed like the right time."

Silence.

Finally, she blew out a breath and resumed cutting his hair as if his touch hadn't affected her. But she didn't fool him. Her hands shook ever so slightly, and her breathing became erratic. She'd felt *it* just like he had.

But what was *it*?

"You didn't answer my question. Will you have dinner with me?"

She continued to snip away, and he hoped he hadn't rattled her so badly that he'd have to wear a hat until his hair grew back out like he'd done in high school when she'd convinced him to be her Guiana pig.

She moved in front of him as she continued to trim his hair, her full breasts at eye level. The brush of her fingers across his forehead sent another wave of desire through him.

"Yes, I will have dinner with you, but I need to go home and shower first, then I'll meet you at the restaurant."

She'd accepted without stipulations—just a simple, slightly breathless yes.

Cassie turned on the hair clippers and shaved the back of his neck, then shut them off and looked at him in the mirror. "Well, what do you think?"

"About what?"

"Your hair, silly. Is that what you wanted?"

He looked at her reflection. He didn't give a damn about his hair. It was Cassie he wanted. "It's fine."

She put a hand on her hip, a sparkle lighting her eyes. "It's fine. Is that the best you can do?"

Her teasing comment drew a smile from him. "You always were demanding," he fired back.

Cassie shook a finger at him before she removed the cape. "I am not demanding. I'm exacting, thorough, methodical."

He climbed out of the chair and tapped the end of her nose. "You are, and it's what I always admired about you growing up—and still do." He paid her, then said, "I'll pick you up at seven."

"I told you I'd meet you there."

He stared down at her suddenly seeing her as a lot more than a *friend*. How had he been blind to this intelligent, beautiful woman all these years?

"I know, but this is a date, and I intend to do it right, so I'll pick you up at seven."

2

Cassie locked the door behind Griffin, not sure what had just happened. They'd been friends since childhood, but never anything more—until just now when he'd invited her to dinner.

Not true.

She ignored the voice. True he'd always been there for her, but he'd always treated like a sister not a woman he was interested in dating until just now. She froze as she was about to sweep up Griffin's hair. What had brought on the sudden interest—her or the boys?

No, he wouldn't do that.

Not intentionally.

The voice whispered through her head, and she couldn't help but think it held merit. Griffin still grieved for his son. And there was no question he connected with Tyler, Trevor, and Jeff. Was it such a leap to think he'd want the boys and *her*—in that order?

She shook her head. She wasn't going there. She was going to have dinner with an old friend that she might be developing feelings for, not a potential mate.

Fresh tears rushed to her eyes, but she blinked them back. No! Crying over Joshua was a waste of time. Time to face facts. She'd wanted him to be the one, but they hadn't been in love. She was upset because he'd found someone, and she was alone—she hadn't even dated since their breakup. Dating had become complicated with three children to consider. Her mother's boyfriends had come and gone in her childhood, and she wouldn't put the boys through that.

She finished cleaning up, grabbed her purse, and said goodnight to her aunt. Before she could escape, Aunt Luella stopped her.

Luella squeezed her bowling pin shaped body out from behind the griddle, swiping a strand of pomegranate-red hair back into her beehive hairdo. Cassie had tried to convince her to change the style for the last decade, but her aunt wouldn't budge.

"Was that Griffin I saw in here earlier?"

"Yes."

"He certainly had a skip to his step when he left."

Her aunt all but rubbed her hands together in gleeful anticipation. Aunt Luella loved to play matchmaker, but Cassie absolutely, positively didn't want her meddling in whatever developed between her and Griffin. She intended to take it slow this time rather than make wedding plans after the first date.

"Did he? I hadn't noticed."

Aunt Luella peered at her over the top of rhinestone red cat-eye glasses. "How could you not see it? It was obvious to anyone looking."

"I wasn't looking."

Her aunt huffed. "Well, you should be. That is one scrumptious man inside and out. And he deserves some happiness."

Cassie couldn't deny that. No one was more deserving of some joy than Griffin Valentine. She pressed a kiss to her aunt's cheek. "Goodnight."

If she didn't leave now, she'd be here until cosmic bowling concluded at midnight. The black lights, loud music, and frenzy of activity was not Cassie's idea of fun, but her aunt thrived on it.

The sun hung low in the sky when Cassie got in her car and headed for home—a modest ranch house with a wrap-around porch just a mile outside the city limits. It had been perfect when she'd purchased it three years ago, but with three boys, what had once been spacious had become confined.

She parked in the garage and walked past the stack of laundry she'd planned on starting this evening and continue to work on all day tomorrow. It could wait. She had dinner plans that beat the hell out of laundry. She just hoped she had something clean to wear.

She breezed into the kitchen and texted Griffin.

Come inside when you get here. I'm running late.

She hit send and didn't wait for a response. Instead, she went straight to the shower. She had a date on Saturday night that wasn't with the laundry. Would wonders never cease?

GRIFFIN ARRIVED A LITTLE BEFORE SEVEN, knocked on the door, then entered as Cassie had instructed in her text. Clothing, sports equipment, and an array of toys littered the normally tidy living room. To say that inheriting three children had turned her neat, orderly life topsy-turvy was an understatement of colossal proportions.

Cassie Cooper thrived on order, but she didn't have a vain or selfish bone in her body. Kind and generous to a fault, those attributes are what drew him to her. Few people would have taken in three children, but Cassie hadn't hesitated. Griffin suspected her reasons had a lot to do with being abandoned herself.

He went to the kitchen and searched the cupboards for a glass. When he couldn't find a clean one, he washed one from the sink, filled it with water and took a long drink, then loaded the dishwasher while he waited.

Cassie came in just as he added soap and turned it on.

"Do you do windows, too?"

Griffin flashed her a grin. "Depends on the pay." He wiggled his brows and was pleased to see a smile light up her features.

"I'll think on it over dinner. Shall we go? I'm starved."

Griffin escorted her to his truck, and ten minutes later they were seated and sipping wine at Little Italy.

Her fingertips brushed over his hand. "This is nice. Thanks for inviting me, but I'm curious as to what brought on the invitation now?"

"Why not now?" He was being evasive, but he couldn't just blurt out he preferred her company to being alone. No woman wanted to hear that. And Cassie wouldn't tolerate such a lame excuse—another thing he admired about her.

The waitress arrived with their food before Cassie could press him further, and by the determined look on her face, she'd had every intention of doing just that.

The moment the waitress left, her gaze pinned him. "How about a real answer?"

Griffin blew out a breath. "We've been friends forever, and I've always liked you, so I decided to ask you to dinner and see if we connected as more than friends."

It was the truth. Maybe not the whole truth, but she didn't need to know loneliness had been a driving factor.

Her smile glowed under the candlelight. "I'm glad you did. I just hope our dinner doesn't ignite a matchmaking firestorm when Aunt Luella hears about it."

"Let me take the doubt out of your mind—Luella *will* hear about it, and she *will* attempt to meddle. What we have to remember is we are adults, and we decide the direction of our lives. No one else."

Cassie's lips twitched. "You say that like you really think that's the case, but you know as well as I do *no one* controls Aunt Luella." She pursed her lips and said, "*No one.*"

His body stirred with desire as he focused on those luscious pink lips. What he was feeling was a whole lot more than friendship. Maybe having Luella Lorraine Lavell nudging him along wasn't a bad thing.

～

"So, tell me about you. Are you glad you moved back to Hope's Crossing?" Cassie asked, when there was a lull in the conversation. She sipped her wine and watched Griffin as he finished his pasta. The man had an appetite that put all three of her boys to shame. She couldn't imagine eating that much food—*ever*.

Gray eyes flickered over her and twinkled with amusement—something she'd rarely seen since his return to Hope's Crossing. Sadness always lurked in his expression—a constant reminder that he'd lost a piece of himself that would never be replaced. Only when he spoke about his job did that spark of the old Griffin return.

"Moving home was the right choice."

"Even though you're not doing surgery anymore."

"Yes, I like family practice, but I'm working with a couple of Sam's players, and they've decided to stay in Hope's Crossing and rehab with me after the season is over rather than go to Chicago. It's not the same as being an orthopedic surgeon, but it still keeps me working with athletes."

Cassie swirled her wine. "Kind of the best of both worlds."

"It is. It's the one thing I missed when I came home. Now I'm working with players, plus, I still have my private practice." He studied her closely. "What about you? Are you happy as a beautician?"

His question caught her by surprise. No one ever asked. Beauty was her calling. She loved cutting and styling hair, giving her customers a new look, making them feel good about themselves, so becoming a beautician had seemed like a logical choice.

"Yes, I am. I know it's not in the same scope as being a doctor, but I love my clients. I love talking to them and hearing what's going on in their lives."

"If you think about it, you're not just a beautician, you're also a counselor."

Cassie considered his comment. "I suppose in the same context as a bartender. There are a lot of lonely people in the world," she said—herself included.

Griffin nodded. "There are. I honestly believe that my time is split between counseling and clinical work. Sometimes what my patients need more than a prescription is just someone to take the time to listen to them."

"The sign of a wise doctor."

Griffin traced a finger across her cheek. "What do you say we get out of here and walk off our dinner?"

The husky tenor of his voice sent a shiver through her. "I'd love to."

A stroll down Main Street sounded perfect, but it pretty much announced they were on a date. Of course, an intimate dinner for two did the same thing. She just hoped Griffin realized what he'd signed on for. While they might consider it a casual date, her aunt and the rest of the community would view it differently.

Griffin paid the bill and escorted her outside. The heat of the day had finally eased. She stared up at the dark sky, where thousands of stars winked down on them.

Griffin's voice flowed over her. "Beautiful night."

"Mm-hmm."

They passed Mumford Theater, the neon lights brilliant against the dark sky. A second-run action-adventure film was playing. How she'd love to see something other than a children's movie.

"We'll have to do a movie one of these days," Griffin said.

"I'd like that."

Griffin threaded his fingers through hers.

It was nice holding hands, really nice, but she wanted his hands in places that had been off limits as friends.

"So why did that video upset you earlier?"

Damn. She'd hoped he'd forgot about that, but of course he hadn't. The man defined tenacity. "Can't we just enjoy the evening?"

He stopped and turned so they were bathed in the glow of the theater lights. "Why can't you tell me about it?"

"Because it was a video of Joshua's wedding, and it doesn't seem like an appropriate topic to discuss on a date with another man."

She didn't want to discuss Joshua. She wanted this evening to be about *them*.

A car drove past as Cassie's gaze locked with Griffin's. She imagined running her hands across those broad shoulders and over that chest that looked sculpted from stone. And that hair! She wanted to do so much more than trim it. She wanted to run both hands through it, feel the silky texture slide through her fingers.

"We were having a nice evening. Could we just rewind and go back to where we're going to see a movie sometime in the future?"

GRIFFIN PROPPED a shoulder against the brick wall of The Wishing Stone, the local jewelry store that belonged to Cassie's cousin, Bella next to the theater. "Now why do I get the feeling that you're trying to change the subject?"

Cassie leaned in and raised up on tiptoe so that her lips were just inches from his. "Did it work?"

Hell yes. She'd sent the blood pumping straight to his groin. He tugged her to him, her breasts nestled against his chest—a perfect fit.

He tucked a wayward strand of flaxen-colored hair behind her ear. "All through dinner, I've wanted to do this," he murmured.

"What? Touch my hair?"

Her teasing laughter drew a chuckle from him, but then he looked into her eyes and saw so much more in the blue depths. The need, the want, the yearning.

His arms came around her, and he lowered his lips to hers. He wanted more than a kiss. He wanted to feel the silky skin beneath her shirt.

Suddenly a flashlight blinded them. "This is an inappropriate display of public affection."

The pretentious voice of Cornelius B. Mumford, Esq., owner of the movie theater, boomed over them—Lord Mumford as they'd called him when they were kids.

"Dr. Valentine, is this really how a professional conducts himself in public?"

It was when said professional was in lust with the woman in his arms. Instead he said, "No sir." Before Griffin could escort Cassie away, Mumford turned to her.

"And you Miss Cooper, you, have children now. Do you really

think this is how a parent should conduct oneself in public? This kind of display has only one place—the bedroom."

Griffin didn't disagree. Not giving Cassie an opportunity to respond, he stepped back, took her hand, and started walking, bidding Lord Mumford goodnight.

Cassie's giggles echoed on the night air as they walked back to his truck. "That man never changes. It's no wonder he and Willa are always at odds."

His niece Willa Dunbar was Cassie's high school friend. "No, he doesn't, but you have to admire that he sticks to his beliefs." He opened the passenger door, and she slid inside.

Instead of driving her home, Griffin headed to Starlight Point.

"Where are we going?" Cassie's voice flowed over him in the dark cab.

"I thought we'd do a little stargazing."

"Where?"

"Starlight Point, where else?"

Cassie's soft gurgle of laughter brought a smile to his lips. "That's so high school."

"What's wrong with that?"

"Nothing. I just thought we'd go to your place."

"And that would have been presumptuous of me, wouldn't it?"

They reached the Point. He shut off the engine, pulled her across the console onto his lap, and kissed her. No soft, delicate, press of lips. It was a full-on attack of mouth and tongue that left them both breathless.

"Griffin."

"Hmmm." He trailed kisses down the column of her neck.

"The gear shifter is digging into my hip."

He smiled. "What do you say we do a little stargazing, then I'll drive you home?"

The last thing he wanted to do was go home alone, but she'd given no indication she wanted to extend the evening. Instead, he slid out of the truck, taking her with him. Setting her on her feet, he grabbed the sleeping bag from the backseat and unrolled it in the bed of the truck.

Cassie's gaze swept over him. "Did you have this planned?"

"I did. I wanted to do something different for our first date."

"This is definitely different."

Cassie hoisted herself into the bed of the truck, but he couldn't tell from her tone if that was a good or bad different.

Once they were settled on the sleeping bag, he wrapped an arm around her. A shooting star jetted across the sky, leaving a trail of stardust in its wake. Was that Bobby signaling he was okay? The idea comforted him.

"You look happy."

"I am. I love stargazing with you."

She fluttered her eyelashes at him. "Griffin Valentine, you sure do know how to woo a girl."

Her comment drew a chuckle from him. "I've never been much of a romantic." Or so Mary had repeatedly told him.

Cassie tilted her head to look at him. "Whoever told you that didn't know what they were talking about. This is one of the nicest evenings I've had in a long, long time." She sighed. "You're easy to be with."

Griffin groaned. "So, I'm the *nice guy*?"

Cassie leaned an elbow on his chest. "I happen to prefer nice guys. They are kind and considerate." She wiggled her eyebrows. "There is nothing sexier in my opinion. Does that soothe your ego?"

He laughed and tapped the end of her nose. "Yes, my ego is appeased."

Her eyes sparkled with merriment, but behind that sadness lurked. He settled her between his legs, her back pressed to his chest.

"So, do you still have feelings for Joshua?"

She released a pent-up sigh. "You're relentless—a dog with a bone. It's not a big deal."

"If that's the case, then tell me about it."

She stared up at the sky, her body tense. Finally, she blew out a long breath. "You really want to talk about my ex?"

Not really, but he wanted to know what had been on that video and why it had upset her.

She leaned into him, and Griffin tightened his arms around her.

"Like I told you earlier, it was a video of Joshua's wedding."

"And you're upset because you still have feelings for him?"

She tilted her head to gaze up at him. "I don't love him. It's just that—"

"Just what?"

She sighed. "I thought he was the one. I thought that would be my wedding." She shook her head. "I'm being silly, I know."

"Not silly, just disappointed."

She smiled. "Yes. Thank you for understanding. You really are a nice guy."

He didn't groan this time, but took it as the compliment she'd intended.

"Is something wrong?" she asked when he remained silent.

How could he begin to explain all that was wrong with him? All the reasons why getting involved with him was a huge mistake. But he didn't.

"No, for once, everything is absolutely right."

She pressed her lips to his. "Thank you for a lovely evening."

Their eyes held.

A shooting star dropped out of the sky.

"Oh Griffin, look." She pointed at it, and contentment settled over him. Something he hadn't felt since before Bobby died, and it was all because of the woman in his arms.

3

E arly the next morning, Cassie's phone vibrated in her pocket. She slowly opened her eyes. The nip of the early morning air chilled her nose and cheeks as the sun inched about the mountains turning thin clouds on the horizon a stunning cotton candy pink.

Where was she?

Her last memory was watching the stars in Griffin's arms, but now she was snug inside a sleeping bag, fully dressed and pressed against one very warm body—Griffin.

She'd fallen asleep on their first date! She wouldn't blame him if he didn't want to see her again. Then again, maybe he wasn't upset if the erection pressed against her back was any indication.

Griffin's rough whisper filled her ear. "Good morning."

"It feels like it could be."

His raspy laugh held the promise of bliss.

Her phone buzzed again. "Sorry. It's probably one of the boys. I need to check it." She took the phone from her back pocket and read the text from Trevor.

Want to come home—now. Come get me.

Trevor *never* asked to come home.

She texted back.

I'll be there right away.

THX.

Griffin nuzzled her neck. "What do you say we take last night to the next level?"

As much as she'd like to do just that, she couldn't. "As tempting as your offer is, Trevor just texted he wants to come home."

"Did something happen?"

"I'm not sure, but he never wants to leave early."

"I'll drive you to Emma and Sam's."

She shifted so they were face-to-face. "Are you sure you want to do that?"

"Why wouldn't I?"

Cassie studied him a long moment. "Where exactly do you see this going, Griffin?"

"Are you talking long-term?"

"I am. I don't do casual, especially with three children to consider." His silence was telling. She pressed a kiss to his lips. "I don't expect an answer right now. Just think about what you want, and we can discuss it further."

She started to rise, but his hand on her arm stopped her. "Is there any reason we can't date and see where it goes?"

"No, there's not, but don't forget it has to be all over town we went out to dinner. And when Aunt Luella gets wind of it, it will bring her matchmaking wrath down on us."

Griffin's laughter warmed her. "I'm not that fragile. I can manage a little meddling from Luella Lorraine Lavell."

Cassie shook her head. She hoped he knew what he was getting into, because she wasn't so sure *she* could handle it, and she'd lived with the woman most of her life.

～

GRIFFIN PULLED up in front of Sam and Emma's house as Cassie combed her hair into a loose ponytail and removed the smudged makeup from the previous evening. Once she finished, she turned her attention to the twelve-year-old sitting on the front porch, smacking the ball into his mitt.

She blew out a beleaguered breath. "I think Trevor is heading into puberty. I am *so* not ready for this."

"What makes you think that?" Griffin asked.

She lifted a shoulder. "I've seen him watching Katy Miller several times when I picked him up at school, and at the bowling alley. They've been friends since he moved here, but I think his feelings have changed. I've tried to talk to him about it, but he just shuts down."

"I could try talking to him if you'd like."

She hesitated. "You're always coming to the rescue. I really need to start standing on my own."

He turned to face her. "Cassie, I know you struggled when the boys first arrived, but you're doing a great job. I'm not trying to imply you need me to step in. I was just thinking Trevor and I could toss the ball around and have a little guy talk."

The tension eased from her body. "I would really appreciate it, but I want to know everything he tells you."

"I'll report back every last detail," he said, then kissed her before climbing out of the truck. Griffin walked over and leaned against the porch railing. Trevor's glum expression said far more than words. "I've got my catcher's glove in the back of the truck. Want to throw a few out behind the barn?"

Griffin stared at the sky, and waited.

Finally, Trevor shrugged and rose.

Cassie climbed out of the truck and met Trevor at the bottom of the steps. "I'm going to see Emma while you two play catch."

"Why didn't you bring your car?" Trevor asked.

Her gaze shot to Griffin's and before she could answer, he said, "We were having breakfast, so I drove her over." It wasn't a total lie. He'd intended to make her breakfast, just *much* later.

Trevor accepted the explanation without question. Probably because his mind was on other things. Then again, Griffin had found that kids preferred simple, honest answers. And it was honest, mostly. But the breakfast he'd had in mind hadn't included food.

Cassie squeezed Trevor's shoulder. "Let me know when you two are ready to go," she said, then went inside.

Trevor watched until Cassie entered the house then followed Griffin over to the truck.

Griffin grabbed his glove, and they headed behind the barn where Sam had built a pitcher's mound and home plate. He'd coached Trevor in spring and summer ball.

"Are you playing fall baseball this year?"

"Yes." Trevor's response was less than enthusiastic.

Griffin understood. Fall baseball just wasn't the same. "It's not like spring and summer is it?"

Trevor grunted, and walked out to the pitcher's mound. He dug his toe into the dirt several times, then faced him and threw a few warm up pitches.

Finally, Griffin squatted behind the plate. "Okay, let's see what you've got."

Trevor wound up and threw the ball.

It landed in Griffin's glove with a heavy thud. The kid had some real potential. "Not bad. Follow through this time."

Trevor nodded, wound up and released the ball.

Whack!

"That's it. Do that again."

Trevor threw several more balls, but his concentration was clearly elsewhere.

Finally, Griffin pushed out of his crouch and walked to the pitcher's mound. "You're not focused. What's going on?"

Trevor slapped the ball into his glove. "It's nothing."

A fat tiger-stripe cat strolled out of the barn and plopped down next to them, rolling in the loose dirt.

Trevor stared at the cat, and Griffin sensed he wanted to open up, so he propped a foot on the fence that separated the pitching mound and the pasture and waited.

"How can you tell if a girl likes you as more than a friend?" Trevor blurted out a moment later.

Griffin restrained the smile that threatened. "Well, there are a few ways to tell. Some will just come out and tell you, which makes it really easy. Others may be a little more reserved—give you looks, send you notes, look for reasons to talk to you."

Trevor's shoulders slumped. "But she's my friend and we talk all the time. How can I tell if she wants to be more than friends?"

The kid really liked the girl. "That's a little more difficult for sure because you'll have to ask her."

His face blanched. "I-I-I can't do that."

"Why not?"

"Because—"

Griffin placed a hand on his shoulder. "I know you'd rather face down a hundred-mile-an-hour fast ball than be rejected by a girl you like, but what if it turns out she likes you, too, and she's just as afraid to talk to you?"

"Couldn't I just text her?"

"You could, but I'm an old school kind of guy. I like to see their expression and judge for myself their reaction. If they don't like me, I'd rather see it, then go off and lick my wounds. And if they do like me, then all the better."

"Is that how you felt when you told Cassie you liked her?"

The kid was sharper than he realized. Griffin had definitely waited a hell of a long time to ask her out. "Yeah, and it felt good to find out she liked me, too."

"But what if Katy doesn't like me in that way?" Trevor whispered.

Griffin squeezed his shoulder. "Then it's going to hurt like hell for a while, but isn't that better than wondering?"

Trevor considered Griffin's question a long minute. "Yeah. I'm just going to ask her and see what she says."

"Girls like brave guys, and telling her how you feel takes real courage. It's the scariest thing I've ever done."

Trevor scratched the cat along the jaw, but he didn't look

convinced. "I'm a loser. Everybody knows I'm the kid whose dad dumped him."

Griffin stilled, his hands curling into fists. He wished Raymond were here right now so he could tell him what a fool he was for leaving his kids. Instead, he took a calming breath.

"You are *not* a loser. Your dad left you with Cassie because he knew she would love you and take care of you—something he isn't able to do right now. And if anyone thinks otherwise, they don't know what they're talking about." He slung an arm around Trevor's shoulders. "You've got plenty to deal with, but the one thing you need to know is, there is nothing wrong with you."

Trevor didn't respond.

Griffin wasn't certain he'd reached him, but he would keep trying until he did.

CASSIE FOUND Emma in the kitchen nursing Annie.

Emma smiled at her, her face soft and serene. Love, marriage, and parenthood agreed with her. And to think just a couple of years ago Emma had despaired over ever finding true love. Now look at her— happily married to Sam Parker, retired professional baseball player and new owner of the Cornhuskers baseball field—the boy she'd loved all through childhood.

Growing up, Emma had always been in the thick of it with Griffin, Sam, and Ryan, Sam's younger brother, but Cassie had never fit in. The truth was, she never wanted to hurt anyone, which hadn't been an advantage, even in a make-believe sword fight.

"What are you doing here already? I thought you'd sleep in and laze around with a free morning," Emma said.

Cassie scoffed as she poured herself a cup of coffee. "Not likely with the mountain of laundry stacked by the washer." She added cream and took the vacant chair next to Emma.

Emma stared toward the laundry room. "Do you think there will ever come a time there aren't three loads of laundry waiting to be washed?"

Cassie laughed. "I think it's an urban legend that we will actually get it under control. And if someone says they have, they're lying or don't have children."

Emma held up her mug of tea. "I agree."

Cassie clinked her mug to Emma's, then took a sip of her coffee. "The reason I'm here so early is Trevor texted that he wanted to come home."

Emma's brow quirked. "Did something happen?"

"No. I think it's about a girl—Katy Miller to be precise, and Griffin's talking to him right now."

Emma's brows arched higher, disappearing into her bangs. "Griffin came with you?"

Cassie held Emma's questioning gaze. "We were about to have breakfast, so he drove me over." It wasn't a exactly lie.

Emma glanced at the clock, then Cassie.

Cassie didn't deny seven-thirty on a Sunday morning was early to be out with Griffin, but most telling were the rumpled clothes she'd slept in. She could see Emma making all kinds of assumptions and even though it was obvious her cousin was dying for details, Cassie said nothing. If she wanted to know, she'd have to ask.

"Ohhh, you are so infuriating. You're going to make me ask, aren't you?"

Cassie grinned as she took another sip of coffee before responding. "Of course. You'd do the same if the situation were reversed." In fact, Cassie had had to grill Emma for information numerous times after Sam moved back to Hope's Crossing. She'd even nudged her in the right direction now and again. She couldn't deny she had a bit of her Aunt Luella's matchmaker blood in her.

"Why is Griffin with you?"

"Because he offered to drive me." She dragged it out intentionally.

"And where was your car?"

"At home."

"Why didn't you have your car?"

"Because I went to Starlight Point to stargaze with Griffin after we went to dinner last night."

Emma took in her wrinkled shirt. "When did you get home?"

"I didn't."

Emma's mouth sagged opened, then she snapped it closed, shock registering in her eyes. "Y-Y-You spent the night with Griffin!"

"Yes, but not like you're thinking."

"So, you didn't have s-e-x?"

She spelled it out as if the baby might understand their conversation.

Cassie rolled her eyes. "Emma, Annie's asleep, and even if she were awake, I doubt that she'd know what we're talking about."

"There are plenty of other listening ears about."

"True, but they can spell—probably better than we can."

"Stop stalling and tell me what's going on."

"I'm not stalling. I'm just pausing for dramatic effect."

Emma growled, "Cassie."

"Okay, don't get your panties in a knot. He asked me to dinner and I accepted."

Emma's grin was brighter than the sunlight streaming in the kitchen window. "It's about time you two got together. You are a perfect match."

"Emma, we went to dinner, that's all."

"What aren't you telling me?"

"I'm just saying we enjoy each other's company, and we'll see what happens." They'd been friends since she first moved to Hope's Crossing, but never anything more. Taking it beyond that made her uneasy. What if it didn't work out and ended their friendship?

~

GRIFFIN DROVE Cassie and the boys home, and while she helped Jeff and Tyler with their homework, Griffin recruited Trevor to help him with the laundry. Cassie heard the washing machine start, then the back door open and close. Several minutes later, Trevor and Griffin appeared in the yard and began mowing the grass. Now how in the world would she be able to go slow with Griffin if he kept doing things that moved him from the *friends* to the *keeper* category?

"Cassie, I'm done. Can I go help Trevor and Griffin?"

Cassie stared at Tyler as if he'd grown two heads. "You want to work in the yard?"

"Can I, please?"

Cassie waved him off. "Go."

"I'm done, too. Can I go out and help?"

"Yes."

"Yippee," Jeff yelled as he raced for the door on Tyler's heels.

She moved to the window and watched as Griffin welcomed the other two boys and immediately put them to work. Every time Cassie tried to get the boys to help her, it always ended in an argument. But as she watched, Griffin deftly redirected the boys whenever tempers flared.

She needed to take notes. She watched Griffin and the boys a moment longer then turned away when something stirred in her belly that felt suspiciously like affection.

4

A week after his date with Cassie, Griffin leaned against the concrete wall above the Cornhuskers' dugout as he listened to Dinger and Dizzy Durant argue over the best way to stop a batter from crowding the plate. The brothers were lean and wiry. What they didn't have in size, they made up for with speed.

"Bullshit. Throwing inside is the best way to make a batter back off," Dizzy insisted, having crowded the plate on more than one occasion during his tenure in the major leagues over a decade ago.

"Unless it's you. You just lean into it," Dinger said.

"Not always."

Dinger hocked a loogie, narrowly missing his brother's size ten shoe.

Dizzy jumped back, glaring at his brother. "You did that on purpose."

A year ago it would have been tobacco not phlegm, but Sam had banned tobacco from the stadium after he purchased the Cornhuskers' field.

A wicked light twinkled in Dinger's eyes. "Just showing you there are other ways to get the batter to stop crowding the plate."

Dizzy scowled at his brother, then stomped off muttering, "I wish you'd take up chewing again."

Griffin chuckled.

Dinger's dark scowl landed on him. "What are you laughing at?"

Griffin held up his hands in mock surrender. "I'm not."

"Damn well better not." Dinger shot him a final glare, then grabbed the bag of gear from the dugout and went into the clubhouse, leaving Griffin alone.

He studied the neatly trimmed turf, the fence covered with shiny new sponsorship signs, batting cages—everything top-of-the-line thanks to Sam. He'd turned the dilapidated stadium into a first-class ballpark. He'd also joined the Midwest Independent Baseball League, so between Liberty Community College and Hope's Crossing High playing here, the field would be in use almost nine months out of the year.

"So what do you think?" Sam asked, coming to stand beside him.

"I think it looks amazing."

"It's even better than I envisioned it, but it's still lacking." Pride resonated in Sam's voice as his gaze made a full circle from the field to the concession stands.

Griffin couldn't imagine what that could be. It looked perfect to him. "I don't see anything missing."

A whoop came from the field as Cassie's boys and Sam's son chased each other around the bases.

Sam stared from the boys to Griffin. "You."

"Me?"

"Yes, you. I need a partner, and I can't think of anyone who would be a better fit. You know baseball and you could act as team physician, but most importantly you love the game as much as I do."

Stunned, Griffin took a moment to mull over the offer. He had no regrets leaving Chicago for Hope's Crossing to take over Pete Townsend's practice, but he missed baseball. When he'd worked as an orthopedic surgeon, he'd been in contact with the players.

"I couldn't give up my practice."

"We can work around your schedule."

The offer appealed to him. He wanted to be part of what Sam was building here.

Sam threw out the buy-in figure for a full partner, and Griffin considered his offer for all of five seconds, then held out his hand. "Deal."

Sam's face broke into a grin. "I'll have my attorney begin drawing up the contract first thing tomorrow. What do you say we celebrate our partnership by testing out the field with the boys?"

Griffin followed Sam down the steps and onto the field, swallowing back emotion as he imagined Bobby out there with them.

"Hey Griffin, pitch to us," Jeff yelled.

He went to the pitcher's mound, and threw until his arm hung like warm gelatin. He didn't care. It beat the hell out of going home where his only companionship was memories of his son.

GRIFFIN CLOSED the office at noon on Fridays, and instead of using the time to catch up on paperwork, he swung by Sittin' Pretty to see Cassie. He'd wanted to come by sooner, but he'd held back after Cassie's pointed questions about where they were going. He didn't have an answer for her. She wanted more than casual dating, but he wasn't certain he could give her that. He'd been a dismal failure as a parent and husband, and he feared he was too much like his father to make any relationship work.

If that was so, why had he asked her out, knowing she wouldn't be interested in a casual relationship? Selfishness. He was tired of eating dinner alone or bumming meals off his friends. He wanted to join the world of the living, and Cassie offered that—light, laughter, and joy, and so much more. It was the more that scared the hell out of him, but it hadn't stopped him from seeking her out.

"Griffin Valentine, I haven't seen you in a month of Sundays. Where have you been keeping yourself?" Luella called out the instant he entered the Beauty Bowl.

"Working." It was the excuse he always used, when in truth he'd been in hibernation.

Hands on generous hips, Luella gave him a once-over, her ever-present baseball cap perched on top of her beehive hairdo. "Don't tell me you're here for another haircut already?"

"No, ma'am."

"Then what are you doing here?"

"Visiting your niece."

Luella waved him over. "Are you smitten with my Cassie?"

He was, but he wasn't sure telling the local matchmaker was the best idea. Instead he kept his response vague. "I've always liked your niece."

She shook a finger at him. "My girl has a huge heart. Don't you break it." Luella gave him a hug that stole the breath from his lungs, then released him. "I know your heart's been broken, but don't let fear keep you from finding love again."

Griffin didn't respond. Instead, he continued on to the beauty salon and found Cassie cutting her cousin Bella's hair.

Griffin straddled the chair that Cassie kept next to the telephone where she scheduled appointments. He'd just seen Bella and Matt a couple of weeks ago when they'd come to him wanting a referral to a specialist. They were in their third trimester of pregnancy and everything was normal, but he could tell Bella wouldn't breathe easily until the baby was in her arms. He couldn't blame her since her first baby had been stillborn. He'd be taking every precaution, too.

"You're looking radiant, Bella."

She flushed all the way to her roots. "That's sweet of you to say, but I think we all know I look like a cow expecting triplets."

"You look absolutely stunning," Cassie chimed in.

Bella glowed under the compliment, and it gave Griffin pause as he wondered what Cassie would look like carrying his child. The image took him aback. It was the first time since losing Bobby he'd thought about more children.

Mary's words rang in his head. *You don't deserve to have children.*

It had taken him a long time to recognize it had been grief and anger she'd been expressing. If only he could believe that in his heart and not just his head.

"Earth to Griffin."

Griffin blinked, and the past evaporated. "Sorry, daydreaming."

Cassie repeated her question. "I asked what you were doing here."

"I came to see if you had time for lunch. And you, too, Bella, if you're free."

"I'd love to, but I have to get back to the shop. I know Cassie's free though because her next appointment cancelled just before you walked in."

Cassie didn't look pleased at Bella's blatant manipulation. "I told you and Emma to stop pushing."

"Why don't I order us something and bring it back here while you finish up?"

Cassie nodded her agreement.

He went out and placed their lunch order with Luella. Sam came in just as Luella went back to prepare his food.

"What are you doing out of the office in the middle of the day?" Sam asked.

"It's Friday. I close at noon, remember?"

Luella stuck her head out the opening between the grill and counter where he and Sam were sitting. "What can I get you?" she called out to Sam.

"A couple of cheeseburgers and fries to go."

"Coming right up."

"So, what's the word on signing the partnership papers?" Griffin asked.

"Probably next week."

Luella came out with Griffin's order. He paid her, bid Sam goodbye, and gave Bella a wave when he saw her leaving the bowling alley. He shouldered open the glass door into Sittin' Pretty and found Cassie on the phone scheduling an appointment. He took their food into the alcove and set it out on the counter while she finished the call.

She sank into the chair next to him and stretched out her legs.

"Long day?"

"The longest. Had a three-hour hair straightening with Marcie Dupree, and she's a yacker—"

"A yacker?" Griffin cut in.

"Yeah, you know, always talking. I don't think she stopped talking the whole time. I even juggled in a cut and style while she was here, and I don't think the other woman said a word other than nodding in response to her. And then I gave Bella a shampoo and cut, and it's only lunchtime."

Griffin pushed her food toward her, then lifted her feet onto his lap. He took off her shoes and socks and began massaging her feet.

"Oh my God, that feels amazing! You should have specialized in massage."

Griffin smiled. "Good to know I've got a backup career if I ever decide to leave medicine."

Cassie groaned when he pressed his thumb into her arch.

"Has anyone ever told you that you have beautiful feet with tiny, perfectly formed toes?"

"You're making me blush."

He laughed. "Hardly. Nothing embarrasses you."

"It's my superhero gift."

Griffin laughed again. "Eat your food. It's getting cold."

Cassie munched on a French fry, then held one out to him. He obediently opened his mouth, and her fingers brushed his lips when he bit into it. He chewed as heat spread through him, igniting a fire in his belly.

Cassie ate another fry. "You know, I don't think I thanked you for taking me to dinner last week and stargazing."

Griffin stopped rubbing and looked at her. "I enjoyed it, too."

Their eyes locked, and Griffin found himself drowning in the blue depths.

"I want you, but—"

"But what?"

"Your friendship means the world to me. I don't want to lose that."

He threaded his fingers through hers. "Neither do I. What if we just spend time together as a couple and see what happens?"

"I'd like that a lot, but it would probably include three boys most of the time."

"That's a given, and just so you know, I love spending time with all of you."

His phone beeped. He took it out of his pocket and saw he had a text from Trevor.

SOS. She said no.

Be there in a minute. He texted back.

"Emergency?"

"Afraid so. Trevor's girl problems are escalating." He'd told her what he'd learned from Trevor the week before and the advice he'd offered.

"Oh no. What happened?"

"He told Katy he liked her, and she didn't reciprocate."

He kissed her, and her fingers curled into his shirt. When he pulled back, she said, "Thank you for helping him through this."

"Anytime. I'll call you later with an update."

She wrapped up his burger and stuffed it back in the bag along with his fries. "You need to keep your strength up when dealing with a preteen." She raised up on tiptoe and kissed him again until they were both breathing heavy.

"Gotta go," he said with real regret. He wanted more than anything to stay with her, but there was a boy with a broken heart in need of a doctor, and he couldn't let him down. Not after Griffin had advised him to go for broke.

G riffin got to the school and found Trevor in the nurse's office complaining of a stomach ache.

"Griffin, who called you?" Tara O'Neal, the school nurse asked. She looked harried, and he saw several kids, pale and on the verge of vomiting, waiting in the hallway.

"I was in the neighborhood. Do you need a hand?"

"Oh my, yes."

"You know, if you ever get tired of working here, I've got a spot for you in my office," Griffin said.

Tara laughed. "If I didn't love my job, I'd be at your door in a heartbeat."

Griffin saw Trevor in the far corner. "Hey, pal, what's wrong?"

Tara answered for him. "He's got a stomach ache. I was just about to call Cassie."

"Why don't you let me look him over before you do that while you check on the others, then I'll come look at them."

Tara thanked him again, then hustled over to a girl who looked ready to revisit her lunch.

Griffin turned to Trevor. "Okay, what happened?"

Trevor hesitated, glancing over at Tara.

Griffin lowered his voice. "It's okay. She's busy and can't hear us."

Trevor cast a final glance at her, then blurted, "I told Katy I liked her. She turned all red, then ran off when the bell rang."

"What makes you think she rejected you?"

His head snapped up, and his eyes darkened with pain. "She didn't say anything after I told her I liked her."

"Have you considered she might be shy and scared just like you? And don't forget you had a chance to prepare, she didn't. You two have been friends for a long time, right?"

"Since Dad left us here. She was my first friend."

"Well, maybe she needs time to think about you as more than a friend."

Trevor shrugged as if his heart wasn't shattered. "You really think so?"

"Give her some time, but here's the big question. If she says no, can you find a way to go back to being just friends? Because good friends are important, and you wouldn't want to lose her."

Trevor gave him a thoughtful nod as Tara called out to Griffin. "I need some help over here."

"Your stomach good enough to go back to class?"

"Yeah."

"Thatta boy. And don't forget, I'm here if you need me, and so is Cassie."

CASSIE CLOSED the shop at three the next day and loaded the boys and her aunt into the SUV, then drove them to Cornhuskers Field for the first game of the playoffs.

Luella twisted around to speak to the boys in the backseat. "Checklist time. Baseball gloves?" She held up her glove.

"Check," all three boys shouted.

"Baseball caps?" She tipped her cap loaded with pins.

"Check!"

"Cleats?"

"Check!"

"Why do we need cleats, Aunt Luella?" Jeff asked, his face puckered in confusion.

"To run the bases after the game."

A smile engulfed his face. "Check!"

Her aunt faced forward. "Looks like we're all set."

Cassie glanced in the rearview mirror. "You've definitely got them all hyped up. Can't tell you how much I appreciate that," she muttered.

"Sarcasm does not become you, Cassandra. It's the playoffs. They should be excited. This doesn't happen every day."

True, but she didn't want the kids so worked up they were out of control and misbehaving either.

They arrived at the field, and the boys scrambled out of the car. They immediately raced for the entrance where Kevin waited for them, a baseball cap tugged low on his forehead, a mitt in one hand, ball in the other, and dusty cleats on his feet.

Cassie got out of the car and followed her aunt into the stadium and up to the reserved seating where Emma and Annie waited for them. It was the perfect spot to watch the game, under cover and with a cat's eye view of the field plus the playground where the boys had gone. It was the best of all worlds—comfortable and cool.

Emma bounced Annie on her knee. "I can't believe you left the salon early. You never do that."

Cassie blew a raspberry on Annie's belly. True, it wasn't her standard mode of operation.

"How could I deny the boys the opportunity to see the playoffs?"

Emma straightened Annie's dress. "Oh, that's a line of malarkey. You could have sent them with Aunt Luella. What's the real reason you're here?"

Cassie scanned the field checking on the boys while keeping an eye out for Griffin. "I'm here to watch the game. Ask Aunt Luella."

Emma turned to their aunt.

Luella didn't look up from the program she was reading. "She's here because she wants to see Griffin," her aunt said, her voice loud enough the people three rows down could hear.

A triumphant grin crossed Emma's face. "I knew it. Cassie's got *a thing* for Griffin."

Her sing-songy voice grated on Cassie. "You sound like a ten-year-old. We went on one date."

"But you'd like it to be more than one date."

She definitely wanted more than a date.

Matt escorted Bella up to them, her belly leading the way. He settled her into the seat between Cassie and Luella.

Luella took off her cat-eye sunglasses and studied Bella closely. "I thought you were going to stay home and rest."

"I'm tired of resting and being at home. Sitting in the stands for a couple of hours won't hurt."

"She insisted on coming," Matt said. He squatted down in front of his wife. "Do you need anything?"

"I'm fine. Go to the dugout. I know that's where you want to be."

Matt brushed her belly, then leaned in and softly kissed her lips. "Text me if you need anything—*anything*," he stressed, then turned to Cassie and Luella. "If she gets tired and needs to go home and rest, text me."

Bella scowled at him. "I am perfectly capable of making that decision."

Matt tapped the end of her nose. "You are, but you won't."

She didn't deny his statement, but clearly she wasn't pleased.

Matt rested his hands on the arms of her seat and kissed her again. "I love you, and I'm just trying to take care of you and our baby."

Tears welled in Bella's eyes, but she rapidly blinked them back before shooing him off. "Go on."

"I still say you should be home resting," Luella muttered under her breath.

Aunt Luella believed rest cured everything.

Luckily for Bella and Cassie, Luella's attention was diverted to the field as the players began to warm up. She forgot about the baby,

Cassie, and Griffin. Her entire focus moved to the upcoming game. And predictable as clockwork, she grabbed her bag and program and went to the third baseline, where one of the up and coming players warmed up.

"Yoo-hoo," Aunt Luella called.

Earlier in the season the players hadn't known how to react to her aunt. Now they welcomed her with open arms.

Bella snorted out a laugh. "I remember when Aunt Luella did that to Matt for the first time."

"He handled it a whole lot better than most of the players, if I recall. You never forget their look of terror when she sashays up to them and starts giving them pointers," Emma said.

Bella held out her arms to Annie, who reached for her. "Boy, isn't that the truth. But then they find out she actually knows what she's talking about."

Cassie listened but didn't participate in the discussion as she watched Jeff and Tyler start to do battle. She pushed out of her seat, ready to head down to the playground when Griffin appeared and took control of the situation with a smile and a few quiet words.

"That man certainly has a way about him," Bella said.

"Mm-hmm," Cassie murmured.

Emma cast a knowing glance at Bella. "She's smitten."

Cassie ignored them. Commenting would only encourage them.

The teams lined up for the National Anthem, and Cassie rose with her cousins, keeping a close eye on the boys to make sure they stood and faced the flag. They did, but with Sam's encouragement.

Griffin stood on the pitcher's mound, a microphone in his hand as he sang the National Anthem.

A chill swept over Cassie as his deep baritone vibrated through her. She'd forgotten what a magnificent voice he had.

The game began, and Aunt Luella returned to her seat, her entire focus on the game, furiously scribbling notes. Cassie was grateful her cousins had turned their attention to the game rather than grill her about her relationship with Griffin.

GRIFFIN LOOKED for excuses to be out of the dugout during the game so he could look into the stands and catch a glimpse of Cassie. He thought he was being subtle, but the hoots and whistles from the team said otherwise.

Sam leaned against the fence beside him. "You know there's no reason you can't go sit in the stands with Cassie."

Griffin cast a sidelong glance at his friend. "I'm aware."

"Just making sure."

"You're a true blue friend."

Sam's laughter echoed back as he went inside the dugout.

Griffin actually enjoyed the ribbing from the team and Sam. It was refreshing to be treated like everyone else, not someone they had to handle with kid gloves.

They narrowly won the game. Griffin ran out on the field with the team, and moments later the stands cleared. He searched the crowd for Cassie and finally caught sight of her talking to Tyler.

"I don't care if he dared you. You don't jump off the top of the bleachers. You could have been seriously injured."

"I'm fine. It's no big deal." Tyler's response bordered on insolent.

Cassie's jaw worked, and Griffin watched as she controlled her temper. "Tyler, I can see you're okay this time. What I'm trying to impress on you is that you should be making these decisions, not allowing your brother to goad you into doing things that aren't in your best interest. Do you understand what I'm saying?"

Tyler nodded, clearly just to appease her. "Can I go out on the field with the team?"

Cassie released a pent up sigh and waved him off.

He rushed past Griffin to join his brothers celebrating the win with the team.

"He's going to turn me gray before I'm forty," Cassie muttered as Griffin came up to her.

He chuckled. "You look like you took the brunt of his stunt."

Cassie ran a hand through her hair. "I did."

"He survived, and he'll hopefully make better choices next time."

"Do you really think so?"

Griffin draped an arm over her shoulder. "Not likely. Do you remember when Sam dared me to jump off the shed roof when we were ten?"

Cassie pressed her lips together, preventing a smile from forming. "I remember. He told you if you wore the red cape you'd fly just like Superman."

"And if you'll recall, I didn't and broke my arm. And if you'll also recall, it didn't stop me from taking another dare."

"You were a slow learner."

Griffin hugged her close. "Lucky for you, Tyler is smarter than I was."

Cassie looked up at him. "I hope you're right, but I just have this sense it goes deeper than refusing a dare from his brother."

"What do you mean?"

Cassie shrugged. "I'm not sure. Just a gut feeling there's something more bothering him."

"Parental intuition is a powerful thing, and it would be foolish to ignore it."

"I'm still new at this, so it's hard for me to tell if it's inexperience or instinct."

"You'll have a misstep now and again, but every parent does. You care about your boys, and you're doing the absolute best you can for them. That's all you can do."

"You always make me feel like I can do anything. I can't tell you how much that means to me."

Griffin's arm circled to her waist and he kissed her. Her soft sigh made him wish they were alone, but since that wasn't going to happen, he said, "What do you say to pizza with the team?"

Jeff walked up at that exact moment and let out a delighted whoop. "We're going to pizza," he yelled.

Griffin smiled, pleased that he wouldn't be having dinner alone.

"I hope you're ready for this."

"For what?" He knew what she was referring to, but wanted her say it aloud.

"For total and complete chaos."

Cassie and pandemonium were just what the doctor ordered.

6

W hile Tyler and Trevor brushed their teeth, Cassie tucked Jeff in. She pressed a kiss to his forehead and was about to turn off the lamp when Jeff's question stopped her.

"Cassie, when is Dad coming to get us?"

An ache built in her chest. At first, Raymond used to call the kids several times a week, then every other week, and now it had been three months. His pattern was eerily similar to her mother's, only she'd quit calling over a decade ago. Cassie hadn't heard from her except the occasional letter saying she'd gone into rehab again—just like the one she'd received six months ago.

Cassie focused on Jeff and answered his question the same way her aunt had with her. "I don't have an answer to that. I do know deep down he wishes he could be with you, and he misses you very much."

"I miss him, too."

Another stab to her heart. "I know." She couldn't promise Raymond would come for him soon or if ever, because she knew how desperately Jeff would cling to that. She'd always been grateful Aunt Luella hadn't given her false hope.

A snort echoed from the doorway. "He's not coming back. He's glad to be rid of us."

Her gaze shifted to Tyler as he climbed into bed across from his brothers.

"Is not."

"Is too."

Cassie shushed Jeff, then went over and sat on Tyler's bed. He scooted closer to the wall. "You don't have to believe this, but he does love you very much."

Another derisive snort. "Funny way of showin' it."

"I know it doesn't look that way, but he does."

Tyler peered over his shoulder at her, and his expression begged her to convince him she spoke the truth. "How do you know that?"

"I've known your dad most of my life. He loves you."

Suspicion filled his eyes. "If that's so, how come he left us here?"

Cassie leaned closer and lowered her voice. "Because he knew this was the safest place for you until he can get back on his feet."

Anguish filled Tyler's eyes. "Why does he have to get drunk all the time? Why can't he be like you and Griffin?"

Cassie knew he'd reject her touch, but she didn't care. She gathered him into her arms and held him close. He struggled a moment then relaxed into her.

"Your dad is in a lot of pain right now. He left you with me because he knew he wasn't being the parent he should be."

"I miss him so much," he said, his voice garbled against her shirt.

She rubbed his back. "I know you do, but no matter what happens you'll always have a home here."

Tyler pulled back, his eyes damp and red. "You swear?"

"I do."

He relaxed and laid down.

Cassie pressed a kiss to his forehead. She would do everything in her power to give all three of them the love and support her aunt and uncle had given her.

～

CASSIE WAS JUST ABOUT to close up the shop three days later when the door opened and a man entered. Not just any man—Chet Cooper, retired Hall of Fame shortstop, aka, the Sperm Donor—as she'd called the man who'd abandoned her mother and never seen his daughter.

This man was not her father. A father didn't deny the existence of his child. Yes, he and her mother had had a one night stand back when he'd been a minor league baseball player, and she'd been conceived as a result. That didn't give him the right to deny his part in it, or to leave her mother to fend for herself. Unforgiveable!

"Hello, Cassie." He towered over her, still all brawn and muscle for a man in his early fifties.

She pulled her wits about her and glared at him. "What are you doing here?"

"I came to see my—"

She held up a hand. "Stop right there. I'm not your anything."

He froze and swallowed, his Adam's apple working. "I'm sorry. I shouldn't have said that. Could we sit a moment and talk?"

"About what?"

"Your mother."

Her mother. Another parent who'd abandoned her. She gestured to the pair of chairs near the entrance. She waited until he was settled before asking, "What about Mom?"

He was silent a long moment. "About six months ago she sent me a letter."

A letter like the one still on her desk. Coincidence? Doubtful.

Cassie carefully schooled her emotions and waited for him to continue.

"Amber told me she'd gone into rehab two years ago for a drug and alcohol addiction and had finally gotten her life together."

How many times had her mother done that over the years? So many times that she had a revolving door on rehab.

"Why did Mom send you a letter?"

Chet's gaze held hers, his eyes the exact color of blue as hers. "As part of her twelve step recovery. She'd resisted making amends, and the letter was her way of taking that step."

Exactly the same thing her letter had said except she wanted to see her, and Cassie hadn't responded. "What could she possibly have to make amends for to you? You're the one who abandoned her."

Chet took an envelope from his pocket and held it out to her. "I think you should read it yourself."

Cassie hesitated, a sense of foreboding coming over her. Whatever was in that letter had prompted her father to come see her, and she sensed the information in that envelope would turn her life upside down.

Stop stalling. You're a grown woman.

Her hand shook as she took out the single sheet of paper and immediately recognized her mother's handwriting. It opened with the same explanation she'd seen numerous times about going into rehab and working her way through the program by making amends, but Cassie stifled a gasp when her mother wrote:

Chet, I'm sorry I walked away from you. At the time, I thought it was the best thing for both of us. I was going to be on the road for months, and I was certain this was my big break. Turns out it was one of many times I thought that over the years, but it never materialized.

Four months after I left you, I found out I was pregnant. I tried to contact you, but never got past your PR people. I don't think they believed me when I told them we'd dated, and I couldn't blame them. You'd become a superstar the instant you were called up, and I'm certain they were fielding dozens of calls just like mine.

I finally gave up trying to contact you, mostly because I'd failed where you had succeeded in your career. I was consumed with envy and more than a touch of bitterness, so I had our daughter determined to raise her on my own. Whenever she asked about you, I told her you didn't want us. The lie came easier than admitting my failures. I'm sorry.

Her gaze met Chet's again. "You never knew about me?"

"No, I didn't. I loved your mother, and I was heartbroken when she left me. If I'd known about you I would have—" His expression darkened and his hands clenched into fists. "If I'd have known, I would have come for both of you."

Chet inhaled a deep breath, then relaxed his hands. "I'm sorry. I still get angry when I think about all the wasted years."

She understood. She had plenty of resentment simmering inside.

"Two weeks ago I flew to Idaho to see your mother."

Pins crashed, and a shout of glee filtered in from the bowling alley.

"Wait, I'm confused. I thought you got the letter six months ago?"

"Amber sent it to the PR firm that handles my fan mail. I was traveling so there was a delay. As soon as I read it, I went to see her."

Something in his tone told her it hadn't been a happy reunion. "What happened?"

"I arrived too late. She'd sent the letter from her deathbed. I never got to talk to her. I spoke to the people she'd worked with and went to her grave. She never mentioned you to them so they had no way to contact you. From what they told me, she'd been clean for several years, but all of the drugs and alcohol had taken its toll on her health.

Cassie's heart lurched. After all these years, she didn't think she could feel anything anymore, but she did. She looked away from his piercing stare and watched a group of kids bowling. The familiar clank of the balls and the faint sounds of customers placing orders at the counter soothed her and brought back memories of her childhood spent with an aunt and uncle who'd lavished her with love and affection. But she'd always waited for her mother to keep her promise—*I'll be back for you.*

"They stored her things in case you came for them. She'd told them she had a daughter, but not how to contact you. I found this." He gestured to the cardboard box next to him.

"What's in it?"

Chet shrugged. "It had your name on it. I didn't open it."

She'd go through it when she was alone. "Thank you for bringing this to me." She rose.

Chet did the same. "I'm sorry. I wish things had been different. I wish your mom had—" He broke off. "I'd like to see you again."

Cassie studied him closely, her heart tripping double time. She'd always dreamed of meeting her father and spending time with him, but resentment still festered deep inside. How could she be certain he would have come for her if he'd known the truth all those years ago. "Maybe we could have coffee?"

He took a business card from his pocket. "Call me when you want to meet," he said.

An awkward silence settled between them.

"Thank you for coming."

Cobalt eyes held hers. "I'd really like to get to know my daughter," he said, then left.

Cassie locked up, and went to the kitchen in search of her aunt. She found her making a fresh pot of coffee.

"I could use a cup of that," Cassie said.

As soon as it finished brewing, her aunt poured them each a cup. For once, it was quiet, so they sat at the table in the back corner of the diner.

"Why aren't you headed home?"

"I need to talk to you," Cassie said.

"What about?"

"Chet Cooper. He came into the salon a few minutes ago."

Aunt Luella added cream to her coffee. "What was he doing here?"

Cassie squeezed her aunt's hand. "He came to tell me that Mom died."

Aunt Luella froze. Her hand trembled slightly as she put her cup down on the table. "How? When?"

"Six months ago. Cancer." Cassie repeated everything Chet had told her.

Her aunt's lips trembled. "She sent me a letter that she'd gone into rehab again and was trying to get her life together, but I didn't answer. She'd sent so many over the years I just—"

Cassie squeezed her hand. "I know. I did the same thing. It's not your fault. You couldn't have known."

Aunt Luella took a napkin from the dispenser and dabbed her eyes. "Neither could you."

True, but she should have responded. If Cassie had known her mom was ill, she'd have gone to see her. Why hadn't she said something in the letter?

"Your mom had an amazing talent. It just never worked out for her."

Cassie nodded, but she also recognized that her failures as a singer had contributed to her problems with addiction.

"I need to pick up the boys from practice. Will you be okay?"

"I'll be fine. You go on." Aunt Luella enveloped her in a hug and whispered, "I know she let you down again and again, but don't forget that she loved you."

Bitterness filled her. Why couldn't her mother have loved her enough to get clean? Cassie left the Beauty Bowl in a daze and went to pick up the boys, who were unusually rowdy. But that was actually a good thing because it helped keep her mind off the news of her mother.

After she got them fed and down for the night, she had a few minutes to herself. Undressing, she climbed into bed, then stared at the box from her mother sitting on the nightstand. She lifted the lid and sitting on top was her mother's necklace. Amber had always worn it, and Cassie had loved it.

The topaz stone shimmered in the light as she stared at it. Emotion welled in her throat as tears streamed down her cheeks. A sob broke free, and she buried her face in her pillow.

7

G riffin's phone beeped as he rinsed his dinner dishes. He glanced at his phone and saw Trevor had texted him *nine-one-one*.

What's wrong? Griffin texted back.

Cassie won't stop crying. Don't know what to do.

I'm on my way.

Griffin grabbed his keys and headed for Cassie's. He arrived ten minutes later. Trevor answered the door, and Griffin stepped inside.

Silence.

"I thought you said Cassie was crying."

"She is."

"I don't hear anything."

Trevor led him down the hall to Cassie's bedroom, where Griffin could faintly hear her muffled sobs. He turned to Trevor. "Okay, I've got this. Go on to bed."

"You'll take care of her?"

"You have my word."

Trevor hugged him tight, and Griffin wrapped his arms around him. "It's going to be okay. Don't worry."

"I love her." Trevor swallowed, his blue eyes a replica of Cassie's. "She took us in after Dad left us. I don't wanna see her crying."

"Neither do I. You did the right thing texting me. She'll be fine. Don't worry."

Trevor pulled back then hurried down the hall to his bedroom.

Griffin tapped on Cassie's door and entered, closing it behind him. He sat down on the bed and gently rubbed her back. "Cassie."

Her sobs eased, and she raised red-rimmed eyes to his. "Griffin." She hiccupped. "What are you doing here?"

"Trevor texted me. He was worried about you. What's wrong?"

She threw herself into his arms, her voice muffled against his shirt. "My mother died."

Griffin hugged her close, murmuring soothing words and rubbing her back until the tears subsided. He eased onto the bed, cradling her to his chest.

"How did you find out?"

Her voice softened. "My dad came to the shop just before closing."

"Chet Cooper came to see you?"

"Yeah, can you believe it? He was the last person I expected to walk into my salon."

"What did he say?"

Cassie repeated her conversation with Chet.

Griffin stroked her hair. "What was in the box?"

She showed him a necklace clutched in her fist. "Other than this, I'm not sure. I saw it and—" Tears streamed down her cheeks again. "I couldn't look any farther."

"Did you eat?"

Cassie shook her head. "I'm not hungry."

"How about some tea?" He made to rise, but she gripped his shirt.

"I don't need anything but what you're doing right now."

Griffin tucked her head under his chin and started humming.

"That was one of Mom's favorite songs."

Griffin sang the words from memory, a soft, lilting melody. Cassie's body relaxed, and within minutes she'd slumped against him, falling into an exhausted sleep.

He kicked off his shoes, and pulled the blanket over them.

She murmured in her sleep and snuggled closer, her soft breath warming his chest.

Holding her in his arms felt like he was finally where he was meant to be.

CASSIE SHIVERED. The green numbers on the bedside clock lit up the darkness. Five-thirty. She'd have to get up soon to get the kids ready for school.

"What time do the boys get up?"

Cassie started, then relaxed when she remembered Griffin had come to console her last night. Her stomach twisted when sorrow filled her again. Her mother was dead and never coming back for her.

Griffin gathered her in his arms and pressed her head to his chest. "It's okay. It will get easier with time."

His words calmed her. When her tears were spent, she wiped her eyes on the sheet. She shivered again, and she wasn't certain if it was the cold or grief that had her trembling.

"I feel like I should make you breakfast for staying with me last night, but it wouldn't be much with my limited skills in the kitchen."

She could feel his smile against her neck. "Another time. I need to get home and get ready for work."

He kissed her, his fingers twining into her hair.

She pressed into him, taking everything he offered.

When he pulled back, they were both breathing heavily. She really wanted him to stay for more than just the comfort he offered.

"I've missed you. I'd really like to see you again. Maybe I could get Emma and Sam to watch the boys," she whispered.

His lips left a trail of kisses down her neck, then back to her mouth. "Or maybe we could all do something together," he said.

She brushed her fingers across his cheek. "I'd like that."

"I'll stop by later and we can make plans." He gave her one last kiss, then he was gone.

Her heart thudded. Griffin was the kindest, most thoughtful man. He came to comfort her last night with no expectation of anything else.

As much as she'd like to move their relationship to the next level, she wasn't sure he was ready to let go of his past. And until he did, she'd only be setting herself up for heartbreak.

CASSIE'S GRIEF came in waves over the next few days. One minute she'd be fine, the next a song on the radio would set her off, or she'd see a mother and daughter together and her eyes burned with unshed tears.

On Monday, she drove the boys to the school, then stopped for some much needed groceries. She was just loading the car when a huge white lab came up to her and leaned against her side. He gazed up at her with adoring eyes and whined. She rubbed his ears.

Pressing closer, he lifted his head to give her access to his neck.

"What's your name, big guy?" She'd always loved dogs and had been considering one for the boys but hadn't done anything about it.

"This is Rookie."

Cassie looked up to find her father beside her.

They stared at each other for a long moment. Finally, he gestured to her necklace. "Your mother loved that. She never took it off."

"I remember." Cassie traced her finger over it. "I always wondered where she got it."

Chet cleared his throat. "From me."

The significance of its origin slammed into her. "Oh." Cassie paused. "I'm sorry I didn't call. I didn't expect Mom's death to hit me so hard."

Chet's gaze softened. "I understand. I cared about your mother, and I'm sorry she's gone. I wish it had been different between us."

Rookie whined, and nosed her hand. Cassie stroked his head. "Thank you for coming and bringing me Mom's things."

"You're welcome. I'm going to be throwing out the first pitch at the game on Friday night at the Cornhuskers game. Will you be there?"

Cassie laughed. "Of course. The whole town will be there. This is a huge event, especially with the team going to the playoffs for the first time."

"Maybe I'll see you there." He signaled Rookie with a soft whistle. "Come on, boy. Cassie needs to get home."

Indecision warred within her. Did she really want to risk her heart with this man who'd only been her father biologically? Before he could step away, she touched his arm.

He froze, his gaze locking with hers.

"We'll be going to dinner after. Would you like to join us?"

A smile slowly spread across his face. "I'd like that very much. Thank you."

She watched them walk down the street. As a child, she'd never been interested in baseball except when Chet played. Every time his team was on television, she'd been glued to the set, and all her make believe games had focused on him coming for her. Now, she was going to a baseball game with Chet Cooper. Would wonders never cease?

CASSIE ARRIVED home ten minutes later, put the groceries away, then started cleaning house. She'd been putting it off, and it desperately needed a thorough scrubbing. She stripped the sheets from her bed and turned for the door. She stopped when she saw the box from her mother on the dresser. She'd been avoiding it, but every time she saw it, it taunted her, tempted her to peek inside.

Open, open, open.

But Cassie didn't want to look inside of what would surely upset her, so she went to the laundry room instead. She'd open that blasted box when she was damn good and ready.

She spent the morning dusting, vacuuming, and scrubbing toilets, but all she could think about was the box on her dresser. Finally, she took a break and carried it into the kitchen. She poured a cup of coffee, then sat down at the table. Gathering her courage, she lifted the lid.

Her heart melted.

She carefully laid the handprint turkey she'd made in kindergarten on the table, then her kindergarten picture and a picture of her and her mom together, smiling and happy. She looked back into the box and saw a manila envelope with her name on it. Cassie opened it and found several letters inside. She picked up one and began reading.

Cassie if you're reading this, it means I'm gone. I'm sorry for so many things. I tried to make amends, but I didn't know where to begin. I failed you so many times I lost count. I'm sorry I lied about your father. I'm sorry I left you. I hope that you'll be able to forgive me for leaving you.

I always put my wants and needs first. The only selfless thing I did was leave you with Aunt Luella and Uncle Albert. I know they gave you a home and a good life—a life I couldn't provide for you. I'm so sorry for hurting you.

Love Mom.

Cassie's hand shook as she set the letter aside.

She shoved everything back into the box and carried it to her bedroom. All those years she'd waited for her mother to come for her, would have given anything to see her again, and now she was gone. It wasn't fair.

Why couldn't you have chosen me over the drugs?

8

F riday afternoon Cassie took her usual seat under the covered section at the Cornhuskers field for the first game of the play-offs. The September sun was relentless, and Cassie was glad they sat under the covered section.

She spotted Chet and Rookie on the sidelines with Sam and Griffin. Rookie accompanied him to the pitcher's mound and waited patiently as Dizzy Durant, the voice of the Cornhuskers, as he called himself, introduced them. "Folks, let's give a big Cornhuskers welcome to hall of fame shortstop, Chet Cooper, and his sidekick Rookie for throwing out the first pitch."

Chet wound up and fired the ball to the catcher, crouched behind home plate.

The crowd cheered and applauded.

The game started and got off to a rocky start when the Cornhusker's star pitcher, Peter Dunning, gave up four runs the first inning. The Cornhuskers battled back with three runs, so Dunning started the second inning only one run down. But the second inning was a repeat of the first. He hit a batter and walked the next one. The third bunted and advanced the runner. Dunning managed to strike out the next batter and the next grounded out.

"This is going to be a long game," Aunt Luella muttered.

Cassie nodded her agreement, and Emma chewed a fingernail to the nub while Annie slept peacefully on her shoulder. Cassie glanced over at the playground where the boys were playing in the creek that flowed behind it. Calling it a creek was a stretch considering the trickle of water that ran through it this time of year. It was more of a mud hole.

She could just see the top of Jeff's and Kevin's heads as they searched for frogs. Her gaze swept the playground for Trevor and Tyler. She found Trevor sitting on a swing with Katy Miller beside him.

Trevor stared at Katy with what looked like adoration. So sweet and terrifying at the same time. *My god, what do I know about prepubescent boys? Not a damn thing!*

Suddenly, Trevor whipped his head to the side, and she followed his gaze to Tyler, who sat on the slide, clearly mocking his brother and Katy. Each day that passed, Tyler became more and more challenging. She didn't need a psychology degree to know he acted out in response to Raymond's abandonment. But neither did that mean she could allow him to continually torment his older brother.

She was about to intervene when Griffin stepped out of the dugout and called Tyler over.

He ignored him, so Griffin called him again.

Finally, Tyler got off the slide, gave his brother a parting shot, then went over to Griffin.

Cassie could see the scowl on Tyler's face. He was not happy, but he listened to Griffin, then a grin spread over his face, and he followed Griffin into the dugout.

Emma elbowed her. "Clever man."

For sure. He'd defused the situation and made Tyler's day by inviting him to sit with the team. The man never ceased to amaze her.

~

An hour later Kevin and Jeff raced up the stadium steps, covered in dust and mud. "We're hungry," they announced in unison.

All Cassie could see of Jeff's face were the whites of his eyes. Everything else was covered in mud.

"What happened to you?"

"I slipped and fell in the creek trying to catch a bullfrog."

Cassie hid a smile. "Go wash up while I order you both burgers."

Jeff held up his hands. "It's only my face that's dirty."

Cassie looked at the layer of grime encrusted on his fingers. "Maybe so, but your mouth is covered with mud. Go wash your hands and your face." She pointed to Jeff and added, "with soap."

Jeff muttered and complained but left to do as she asked.

Emma gave Kevin the same instructions. He also protested as he trudged off after Jeff to the restroom.

"Do you suppose there's nutritional value when there's grit mixed in with their food?" Emma asked.

Cassie laughed. "I don't know, but I'm betting those two have had a fair amount of it over the years."

Emma gestured to Annie, who was awake and grinning. "I think she's already got a head start."

A layer of grime covered the baby. "How is this possible? She's been sleeping on your lap until just a few minutes ago."

Emma shrugged. "I have no idea. All I know for sure is if there's dirt around, she'll find it—or it finds her." She held out Annie. "You hold her, and I'll go get the boys their food."

Cassie smiled and took the baby. "Deal." She sat next to her aunt who had ignored the exchange, Luella's entire focus on the game. "Let's go, team!" She clapped and whistled, prompting Annie to clap.

Cassie turned Annie to face her and bounced her on her lap. "You're going to be a baseball player just like your brother and cousins, aren't you?"

The baby gave her a slobbery grin and patted Cassie's face.

"Strike three," the umpire shouted.

Aunt Luella turned to her. "Watch my things. I'm going to give Dunning a pep talk."

Cassie started to suggest that might not be a wise idea, but her aunt was already clomping down the steps. Instead, Cassie sent a nine-one-one text to Griffin warning him Hurricane Luella was about to blow in.

GRIFFIN GOT Cassie's text after Luella had Dunning cornered and was giving him pointers to improve his game.

Tom McCarthy, their head coach, had been pacing most of the game in between shouting instructions to the team and arguing with the umpire. Generally calm, Tom was on edge about this game. The Cornhuskers were the favored team and had a far better record, but they were playing like a last-place team, and Tom's frustration was obvious.

Tom spotted Luella above the dugout and made a beeline for her. "Luella, you know the rules. No talking to the team while we're playing. You can give them all your Bull Durham B.S. after the game."

Luella puffed up with indignation. "I know more about this game than some loose woman from an overrated movie."

Griffin hid a smile, because that was Tom's favorite film and Luella knew it.

"I don't have time for this. Leave now or I'll ban you from the dugout."

Luella's eyes narrowed. "You wouldn't dare."

Tom climbed on the bench so they were nose-to-nose. "You really want to test me on that?"

Luella put on her glasses and gave him a hard stare, not backing down. Before it escalated, Griffin intervened. "Tom you've got a game to coach. Why don't you let me handle this?"

Tom glared at Luella a moment longer then turned back to the game.

Griffin lowered his voice so only Luella could hear him. "He's under a lot of stress. Why don't you text me any suggestions, and I'll relay them for you?"

Luella's gaze hardened as she stared at Tom's back. She raised her voice. "Stubbornest man in ten counties. I could help, you know."

Tom grunted, indicating that he'd heard her but didn't turn around.

Griffin lowered his voice as he tried to placate her. "I know you can help. That's why I asked you to text me."

Luella remained silent a long moment then gave a single swift nod. "All right, I'll text you." She shook a finger at him. "But you'd better pass on my suggestions."

He crossed his heart. "I swear."

Appeased, she turned and headed back to her seat.

Dunning edged up to Griffin, his eyes on the coach. "You know, her suggestions do help."

"Dunning, get your head in the game," Tom snarled without turning around.

He and Griffin shared a look that said Griffin would pass on any texts from Luella.

The Cornhuskers scored two more runs, which put them in the lead heading into the fifth inning. Dunning took the field again to everyone's surprise, including Griffin. Luella texted him throughout the inning with suggestions for Dunning that he promised to share as soon as he came off the mound.

Tom glanced at him, his dark eyes clouded with anger. "Are you texting with Luella?"

"Yes."

"Why?"

"So that you can stay focused on the game."

Tom looked back to the pitcher's mound, then grunted. "Thanks. The woman knows her baseball, but—"

"It's distracting right now?"

"Yeah." Tom took an antacid tablet from his pocket and thumbed it into his mouth then rubbed his arm.

Griffin studied him more closely. Exhaustion ringed his eyes. "Are you feeling okay?"

Tom didn't look away from the game. "I'm fine. Just worried about winning."

He didn't look fine to Griffin.

Tom popped another antacid.

Griffin took Tom's wrist to check his pulse.

Tom swung around to face him, pulling away. "What the hell are you doing?"

He swayed, and Griffin grabbed him, easing him onto the bench. Tom's face tightened with pain and pressed his hand to his chest.

"Hand me my bag," he shouted to the player next to him.

Griffin yanked it open and grabbed a bottle of aspirin. "Take this," he said, while he called for an ambulance.

"What are you doing?" Tom gasped.

"Saving your life."

THE PARAMEDICS LOADED Tom onto a gurney, and Dizzy announced, "Cornhusker fans, will you rise and wish Coach McCarthy a speedy recovery?"

The fans stood in silence as Tom was carried off the field, Griffin at his side.

Cassie watched until they disappeared from sight then looked back at the dugout, where Chet stood with Rookie beside Dinger.

"Folks, now let's give a round of applause to Chet Cooper and the phenomenal Rookie who are filling in for Coach McCarthy," Dizzy said.

The crowd went wild when Chet tipped his cap at the stands and waved, Rookie glued to his side.

Cassie released an enthusiastic cheer. That was her dad down there and she wanted to shout it out to the world.

The game resumed, and Dizzy's voice came over the loud-speaker. "Folks, we have a new bat boy, Rookie. According to Coach Cooper, this isn't Rookie's first time on the field. He's been to dozens of stadiums, and I'm told he also loves to visit the stands between innings. Be sure and give him an attaboy when you see him."

The game resumed, and the Cornhuskers first baseman, Danny O'Malley, walked.

Emma pointed to the field. Rookie trotted out, tail wagging furiously, picked up the bat and carried it to the dugout.

When the team took the field, Rookie came into the stands, and the kids crowded around him, feeding him treats and giving him plenty of love. Obviously, he'd done this many times before.

He made his way up to Cassie and plopped down beside her, his tail thumping against the wood floor and with what appeared to be a grin on his face. He leaned against her, staring up at her with adoring eyes. She stroked the silky fur, then looked down at the field, where Chet stood studying her. Their eyes locked before he turned his attention back to the game, but Cassie knew he'd sent Rookie up to her.

Whenever the team was in the field, Rookie made his way into the stands and plopped down next to her. The kids crowded around him, but he never moved from her side until the team came to bat, then he trotted back to the dugout and fetched bats to the delight of the fans.

The Cornhuskers squeaked out a win, and the crowd surged to the field.

"I think Griffin has some competition," Emma teased when Rookie came up to her.

Cassie stroked his head and couldn't disagree.

9

Griffin met Sam the next morning at Cornhusker Field. They had to win one more game to make it to the championship game, and their head coach was in the hospital recovering from a heart attack. They'd been fortunate Chet had been willing to step in for Tom. No question he'd been a big contributing factor to their win, and Sam and Griffin were hopeful he'd agree to coach the rest of their games.

Chet arrived with Rookie at his side. He signaled the dog, and he sat.

Sam didn't waste any time with idle chitchat. "As I'm sure you're aware, our head coach is out for the rest of the season and perhaps longer. We were hoping you and Rookie might consider replacing him."

They knew it was a long shot getting a superstar like Chet Cooper on board, but they had to try.

"Actually, I was hoping that's why you asked me here."

Sam's eyebrows shot up. "Really?"

"Yes. I've decided to stay in Hope's Crossing for the immediate future, and I need something to fill my time. This will be perfect."

Griffin and Sam exchanged a look and grinned. "We can't tell you what a relief it is to hear that," Sam said.

They discussed the terms and came to an agreement. When they were finished, Griffin asked, "So, what made you decide to stay?"

"I want to spend some time getting to know my daughter." Chet paused, his gaze moving to the huge glass window that overlooked the field. "I miss baseball, too."

Griffin understood. He'd felt the same way after he gave up surgery to come here. Being an orthopedic surgeon had given him a connection to baseball, but becoming a partner in the Cornhuskers had helped fill that gap.

The men discussed the upcoming game and the practice schedule, then Sam and Griffin showed Chet and Rookie around the stadium and Chet's new office. They gave him the keys to the gates before they broke up an hour later.

Griffin climbed into his truck, but didn't start the engine. He'd had dinner with Cassie and most of Hope's Crossing after the game last night. Tonight he was back to his old routine of grabbing takeout and eating alone.

What he wanted was dinner with Cassie without a baseball team in attendance. He grabbed his phone and called her.

"Hi Griffin. What's up?"

Her voice filled up all the empty spaces within him. He settled back against the seat as the loneliness eased. "I was wondering if you'd made plans for dinner yet."

"Actually, I haven't."

"What would you say if I came over and made you and the kids dinner?"

"I'd say the boys would think you're Superman, since I'd planned on leftovers."

He drew in a breath and suddenly felt as vulnerable at Trevor. "And what about you? What would you think?"

"I never refuse a dinner that I don't have to prepare," she joked, then her tone turned serious. "I'd also really like to spend time with you."

"Then it's a date. I'll bring the food and make dinner." He waited for her agreement, then said, "See you at five," and disconnected the call.

THE INSTANT GRIFFIN ended the call, Cassie's phone rang again. Assuming it was him, she said, "Hey, good looking. Did you forget something?"

"No."

"Raymond." Emotion knotted in her throat.

"Yeah, it's me. Who the hell is good looking?"

Cassie ignored his question and asked one of her own. "How are you?"

Silence, then, "I didn't call to talk about me."

"Why did you call?"

"To check on the boys."

"They're doing well. They miss you and ask about you all the time. They want to know when they'll see you again."

An impatient snort came over the line. "I can't just run to Hope's Crossing to see them."

Cassie softened her voice and curbed her annoyance. "Why not?"

"I just can't."

"I could come and get you or bring them to see you."

"No!" A long, weary sigh accompanied his outburst. "I'm sorry. I shouldn't have shouted. I don't want them here. I don't want them to see me like this."

Meaning, he didn't want any of them to see the circumstances he'd fallen to.

"Raymond, you have options."

Another snort. "Like what?"

"Rehab."

"I've tried it. It doesn't work."

"Then try again and again until it does. We want you to get better."

"We. Who is this we? Nobody gives a shit about me."

"Not true. I do. Aunt Luella does, and so do Emma and Bella."

"You're all pushovers and care about everyone."

"We're not pushovers. We're your family. We love you and want you to get well. Let us help you."

A beat of silence then, "I can't do it, Cass. I can't face letting everyone down—again."

"This is your life we're talking about. You have to keep trying."

Another longer pause. "I'm sorry, I can't."

"What about the boys? They need a father, Raymond."

"What about them? They've got you."

"They need more. They need stability."

Something akin to panic filled his voice. "Are you saying they can't stay with you anymore?"

"No, just the opposite. I want legal custody of them."

"*What?*" His voice rose several decibels. "Never. They're mine, and I'm not giving them up."

"Hear me out? The boys need to know they have a permanent home."

"I'm not giving them up!"

"Will you at least think about it?"

Silence, then the line went dead.

When he refused to see them or go into rehab, she'd naïvely assumed he'd let her take custody. Clearly, that wouldn't happen. But the kids needed to know they had a permanent home with her, especially if something happened to Raymond. Unless she took legal steps, they could end up in foster care. She'd been stalling, but it was time she took action. She needed to contact an attorney and find out what she had to do to ensure the boys stayed with her.

The bell clanked, and startled Cassie from her reverie. Her gaze shifted to the door where Chet and Rookie stood. They came over to the desk where she'd been talking to Raymond. Rookie plopped down beside her, his tail thumping with barely restrained excitement.

She forced a smile and pushed her conversation with Raymond aside. Squatting down, she rubbed Rookie's ears. "What are you guys doing here?"

"We have some news."

She looked up at her father. "What?"

"Rookie and I will be staying in town indefinitely."

"Really? Why?"

Chet silently studied her. "I've agreed to be head coach for the Cornhuskers and finish out the season for Tom McCarthy. I've been wanting to get back into baseball since I retired." He paused a moment, then continued, "I miss baseball, and I need something to occupy my time. It seemed like the perfect opportunity."

"Is that the only reason you're staying?"

He hesitated, the blue of his eyes deepening. "No, I'd really like to spend time with you, too."

All her life she'd craved what all the other kids had—parents. She'd followed Chet's baseball career and knew everything about him. But following him online wasn't the same as getting to know the man in person, and now that she had the opportunity to get know her father, she hesitated. What if he didn't live up to the fantasies she'd built in her head?

"I'm glad you're staying. I'd really like to get to know you, too."

Chet nodded. "I was hoping we could start with lunch."

Rookie pressed against her leg and she stroked his silky fur. "I'd like that." She hesitated, then drew in a fortifying breath. "Why don't you come to dinner at my place tonight instead."

Chet's eyes darkened with an emotion Cassie couldn't decipher. "How can I turn down a home cooked meal?"

Cassie wrote down her address and handed it to him.

"Is there anything I can bring?"

"Nope. Just you and Rookie."

"What time?"

"Five."

"I'll see you then." He whistled to Rookie then turned and walked out the door.

～

GRIFFIN ARRIVED at Cassie's with two hefty bags of groceries after she texted that she'd invited Chet to dinner. He took one look at her when he walked in the door, and asked, "What's wrong?"

"I can't discuss it right now. Later, after the kids are in bed."

He hugged her, his voice warm against her ear. "Your mom?"

Cassie shook her head. "Raymond."

He pulled back and looked at her. "You talked to him?"

"Yes, he called right after you did."

"Cassie, I'm hungry," Jeff yelled from the family room.

"I'm starting dinner now," Griffin called back.

"No, you're not. You're sucking face with Cassie," Tyler said from the doorway, his voice insolent.

"I don't care for your tone or that phrase," Cassie said.

The doorbell rang, and Tyler ran to answer it, shouting, "I'll get it."

Moments later Chet and Rookie joined them. Chet handed her a bottle of wine as Tyler and Trevor crowded around Rookie.

"Trevor, it's your turn," Jeff shouted from the living room.

"I'm tired of playing."

Jeff stormed into the kitchen. "You always quit when you're losing."

"Do not."

"Do, too."

"What are you playing?" Chet interjected.

Jeff's mouth sagged, then he recovered. "Major League Baseball."

"Maybe I could take over for your brother?"

Jeff's scowl vanished. "Sure, come on." He grabbed Chet's hand and dragged him into the living room, while Trevor and Tyler took Rookie outside to play, giving Cassie and Griffin some time alone.

Cassie softly pressed her lips to his and murmured, "Thank you for making dinner for all of us. I know it's not an intimate dinner for two."

"It's okay. I don't mind."

" I do. I enjoyed our time alone and would like to do it again. I just couldn't turn Chet away."

"Seriously, I don't mind, but that's not to say I wouldn't enjoy being together just the two of us," he said.

She hugged him, then asked, "What can I do to help?"

Griffin set her to fixing the salad while he prepared macaroni and cheese.

Within minutes the kitchen smelled of warm cheese and pasta, and Cassie's stomach rumbled in response.

The mac and cheese tasted even better than it smelled, and the boys scarfed down their food.

After dinner, Griffin shooed her and Chet into the living room while he and the boys cleaned up the kitchen.

"Griffin is good with the kids."

Cassie smiled. "He is."

"Not many men would handle the three of them so well."

Was he implying he'd have been one of those men? Cassie changed the subject. "So, where are you going to be staying?"

"I'm looking for a house to rent with a yard for Rookie."

"In or out of town?"

Chet shrugged. "It doesn't matter. Do you have something in mind?"

"Actually, I do. One of my customers mentioned their rental is vacant. It's just down the road about a mile east of here. It's a nice place with a big yard and a pool."

"That sounds perfect, but I don't want you to feel like I'm crowding you."

Cassie appreciated his thoughtfulness. "It's okay." She gave him the contact information.

"Thanks. I'll call her tomorrow." He checked the time. "I should go. Thank you for inviting me." He rose and so did Cassie.

"I'm really glad you came. I know it's a little crazy here."

"I don't mind disorder, in fact, it's refreshing. I enjoyed spending time with all of you." Chet paused, then said, "If you need any help with the kids, I'm available."

Cassie remained non-committal. "I'll keep that in mind. Thanks. Boys, Chet's leaving."

They came storming in. "Already," Jeff whined. "I wanna to play another game."

Chet grinned at him. "Maybe we can do it again soon."

"When?"

Chet laughed. "I'm not sure."

The boys crowded around Rookie and petted him goodbye. As soon as Chet left, Cassie herded the boys to bed, then came back to the living room where Griffin waited with a glass of wine.

She sat down beside him and stretched her legs out on the coffee table. "Thank you for dinner and giving me some time alone with Chet."

"I enjoyed it." He handed her a glass. "What did Raymond want?"

She took a sip of her wine while she gathered her thoughts. "To check on the kids, I guess."

She met his concerned gaze. "I tried to convince him to come home and go back to rehab. He flatly refused. Then I suggested that I keep the kids permanently. He blew up and turned me down flat. I tried to reason with him, but he hung up."

He stroked her hair. "I'm not sure anything you said would have made a difference."

Cassie sighed. "I know, but I want to keep them. I can't imagine giving them up now." It surprised her just how much she wanted them, considering how incompetent she'd felt as a parent when they first arrived. "I've always wanted children, but I never pictured myself as an instant parent. Now, I can't imagine life without them."

"Life doesn't always turn out as we expect, does it?"

Cassie snuggled against his chest. "It doesn't, but I've decided to file for legal custody. I hate to do it, but I need to be sure that if something happens—"

Griffin stroked her hair. "You're making a wise decision."

Cassie swirled the wine in her glass, watching it spin from side to side. "I know, but what if the courts decide in his favor? It's not inconceivable that they would side with a parent over a relative. And honestly I feel guilty taking them away from him, but I have to do what's best for the kids. I don't want them to end up in foster care because I didn't want to hurt Raymond. I should have gone to the authorities when he left them, but I just kept thinking he'd come back. And at the same time, I was afraid."

"Of what?"

"That the courts would decide I wasn't competent to take care of them," she blurted out.

Griffin's expression turned resolute. "You can seriously say that? Inexperience is not the same as abandonment. You turned your life upside down for those boys because you love them. That's a whole lot more important than being the experienced parent. The court will also recognize what you've done."

His words warmed her. He always managed to make her feel better.

"I know someone who practices family law. He's good," Griffin continued.

"Thanks. I don't have anyone in mind."

Griffin settled her more firmly against him. The stress of the day began to fade, and she relaxed. She wasn't alone. Aunt Luella, Emma, and Bella would be there for her to lean on, but the one person she really wanted was Griffin. The question was, was he in it for the long haul?

1 0

Griffin pulled into Cornhusker Field right behind Luella. No doubt her early arrival meant she intended to deliver a pep talk to the team. Luella had bought into the team shortly after Griffin and insisted all she'd wanted was her choice of seats and access to the players. But she was a lot more involved than she'd initially indicated she'd be, particularly during playoffs. Neither Sam or Griffin were surprised.

They'd warned Chet about their *silent* partner, and he'd assured them he could handle Luella. Chet was about to discover he'd have his hands full, especially with the determined set to Luella's jaw. She was a woman on a mission and nothing would stop her.

Griffin followed, but had no intention of intervening. Chet was in charge, so Griffin slowed his pace as he followed Luella into the stadium. She headed straight for the bullpen, just as he'd expected.

He met Sam inside. "I see Hurricane Luella has arrived."

Griffin chuckled. "Yup. I was going down to see how Chet handles her."

Sam made a sound that Griffin took as agreement. "I'd like to see that, too."

"There is no handling Luella. She's in charge—period."

Sam's laughter boomed over the near empty stadium.

"So what did you find out in Chicago about our single A status?" Griffin asked as they headed down to the dugout.

Sam's expression switched from amusement to frustration. "A lot of politics. They want us to jump through a bunch of hoops before they give us final approval."

They reached the dugout. Griffin braced an elbow against the concrete wall as they watched the team warm up. "Maybe we should just stay in the independent league."

"I've been considering the same thing, but it could be a struggle financially if we do." Griffin cast a sideways glance at Sam. "I'm not in this for the money. As long we can stay afloat, I don't need an income out of this."

"I don't either, but there's this competitive side of me that wants to be successful financially, too. If we stay independent, we'd have a lot more control."

Griffin understood that need to succeed. It was the only thing that had kept him functioning after Bobby died. "That work is going to fall mostly on you if we stay in this league. I'm fine with hiring on more staff and taking less profit. And I like the idea of maintaining control. What do you think?"

"The same thing. I talked to Tom yesterday. He's resigning, so we're out a head coach."

"Because of the heart attack?" Griffin asked.

"Partly, but he'll be seventy next year, and it was a wakeup call for him. He wants to spend time with the family. His wife wants to travel, and he keeps putting her off."

"And the heart attack was a big reality check," Griffin surmised.

"Exactly. And that leaves us in need of a head coach."

Chet shouted out instructions to the team, drawing Griffin and Sam's attention back to the field, then to each other.

"Are you thinking what I'm thinking?" Griffin asked.

"That we have the perfect head coach right here. Do you think he'd consider taking over permanently?"

Griffin watched as Billy White caught a popup in left field. "He has strong motivation to stay in Hope's Crossing because of Cassie. What do you think it would take to keep him on, financially speaking?"

Sam hitched a shoulder. "I'm not sure, but I say it's worth a try to get him on board. I need to go to the announcer's booth. I'll catch up with you later."

Griffin headed inside the dugout to see if any of the players needed assistance before the game.

Luella's voice carried from the bullpen to the dugout. "Get your arm up and get on top of the ball."

Davis threw a couple of times, then Luella said, "Finish your pitch with a good follow through."

Griffin watched as Chet crossed over to where Luella was handing out advice faster than Grover Clark sucked down beers in the bleacher seats. "Luella."

She shoved her cat-eye sunglasses up onto her forehead and squinted at Chet. "Coach."

There was a long pause as they studied each other. Finally, Chet said, "I assume you heard I'm coaching the rest of the season. The boys tell me your advice has been invaluable to them. Any chance you'd consider sitting in the dugout during the game?"

Luella's smile rivaled the midday sunlight streaming down on her. She pulled Chet in for a hug that Griffin knew from personal experience would squeeze the breath from him.

"I would be delighted to!"

They stood shoulder-to-shoulder and watched Davis warm up, discussing his form.

Chet Cooper was a perfect fit for the Cornhuskers. Now, if they could only convince him to stay on permanently.

CASSIE ARRIVED at the game just after the first pitch was thrown. Fortunately, Emma had picked up the boys for her, or Cassie would have had to listen to their continual complaining when she'd been delayed.

She took her seat next to Emma and Annie, who was wearing a Cornhusker tee-shirt and miniature baseball cap with the team logo on it.

"You're late," Emma said the moment she sat down.

"I know. Can you believe Miranda Phillips came in demanding a cut and style ten minutes before closing? Everyone in town knows this is the championship game, and businesses are closing early to be here."

"You could have said no," Emma reminded her, straightening Annie's shirt.

Cassie sighed. She'd hated missing a moment of the game, especially since Chet was coaching, but when it came to paying clients, she had a hard time turning anyone away. She'd had lean times, and she was always prepared for them. And now that she had a family, money mattered even more. The boys always needed something, whether it was new cleats or money for a school project, and that didn't include her grocery bill that had skyrocketed since their arrival.

"Strike three." The umpire's shout drew Cassie's attention back to the game.

"Where's Aunt Luella?" she asked, suddenly aware her aunt wasn't in her seat.

"Chet made her an honorary coach with a seat in the dugout."

Had he done that to get closer to his daughter? If he had, she resented the manipulation, but she gave the man a silent kudos for such a devious plan. Aunt Luella would definitely be rooting for him from here on out.

"Seriously?"

Emma gave her a single, swift nod. "He didn't do it to make points with you."

Cassie shot a sidelong glance at her cousin. She hated it when she read her mind. "How do you know that?"

Emma shrugged, her attention on the game. "He's the head coach and this is the championship game. He wouldn't ask her just to make points with you. He's got too much at stake to do that."

Cassie couldn't deny she had a point. "Then why do you think he invited her to sit in the dugout?"

A broad smile lit up Emma's face. "If I were to guess, it's because the team considers Aunt Luella their good luck charm. The man's probably superstitious and hedging all his bets."

That made perfect sense. Cassie relaxed and settled in to watch the game, but disappointment filled her. Deep down she'd wanted Chet to go the extra mile for his daughter.

~

LEONARDO'S PIZZA PARLOR teemed with people, but Sam had managed to get the backroom for the team. Cassie and the boys joined them to celebrate winning the championship game. Baseball was over for the season. Cassie was always sad to see the season end, this year more than others because it would mean less time ogling Griffin from the stands.

Rookie rested his head on her knee and stared up at her with those soulful eyes.

And then there was Rookie. The instant she'd laid eyes on him, she'd fallen in love with him. She rubbed his ears. Now that the season was over Chet and Rookie would be leaving.

"Cassie." Jeff's voice brought her out of her reverie.

She focused her attention on him. "Yes?"

"Do you have any quarters? Kevin and I want to play video games."

Cassie fished in her purse and came up with two quarters each. Video games could break the bank, but fortunately Tyler and Trevor had some serious hero worship going on with the team, and not even the lure of video games would pull them away from the players.

"Cassandra, set these two boys straight. Did Meghan Markle have her hair up or down for the royal wedding?"

Cassie shook her head. Only her aunt could get a bunch of baseball players talking about celebrity hairstyles instead of baseball. When it came to hairstyles of the rich and famous, Cassie was a savant. Aunt Luella was well aware of that fact and took advantage of it on more than one occasion.

"Meghan chose not to wear her signature chignon and wavy tendrils. Instead, she center-parted her hair and tucked it behind her ears with a series of coils pinned along the back of her head. And the Queen Mary tiara was placed on top of her head with a veil."

When she finished, the players sitting on either side of her aunt each handed her five dollars.

Cassie gave her aunt a hard look. "You promised you wouldn't take advantage of the players anymore."

They looked at her aunt, clearly shocked such a sweet lady would do such a thing.

Aunt Luella had the grace to blush.

"Give them back their money."

Her aunt glared at her, then relented and handed them back their money.

Griffin straddled the bench beside her, and his voice whispered over her, "I say she should keep it. They should have known better than to bet her."

Cassie faced him. "Perhaps, but do you really want a part owner, even a supposedly *silent* one, placing bets with your players?"

"Okay, point taken, but I'm going to tell Chet he needs to have a discussion with the team about betting—especially with one of the owners."

Cassie looked down the table to where Chet was chatting with Sam and a couple of the players.

Griffin's voice sounded in her ear again. "You could go down and talk to him."

She shifted to face Griffin. "I know, but truthfully I'm still a little in awe of him. He's the superstar baseball player I thought abandoned my mother, then I learn he never even knew about me until a couple of weeks ago. It's just so much to take in."

Griffin's dark gaze probed hers. "It is, but it's also an opportunity you've always dreamed of—to get to know your father."

Rookie whined as if in agreement.

Griffin was right. Even if Chet was only here temporarily she would spend as much time as possible getting to know her father.

∼

A WEEK LATER, Cassie left for Chicago to meet Mark Duncan, the family law attorney Griffin had referred her to. Fall colors flashed past as she headed for the city. October arrived in brilliant color and the days had turned pleasantly cool.

She arrived just before noon, grabbed lunch, then walked to the attorney's office for her one o'clock appointment. She waited only a few minutes before she was ushered into his office.

"Ms. Cooper, it's a pleasure to meet you."

He shook her hand and gestured to the seat across the desk.

She sat down. "Please call me Cassie, and thank you for agreeing to see me so quickly."

"I'm always happy to make time for a referral. Griffin and I go way back. We went to college and played baseball together."

"So you must have known Sam Parker, too."

"Yes, we called ourselves the fearsome threesome back in the day."

Cassie grinned, some of the tension easing from her as they chatted. "I can picture that."

"So, Griffin tells me that you're raising your cousin's children."

"Yes, that's correct."

"Explain the situation to me."

"My cousin Raymond and I grew up together. He was pretty wild until he met Maria in college. They got married, had three boys, then she was killed in a car accident three years ago. Raymond managed for a while, then he started drinking—heavily. About a year ago, he came to visit my Aunt Luella. He asked her to watch the boys for a few days. He'd done that before, but he'd always come back for them. This time he didn't. My aunt is a strong woman, but taking in three young children at her age was more than she could handle, so I brought them to live with me."

"How old are the children?"

"Trevor is twelve, Tyler's ten and Jeff's nine."

"And you're single, is that correct?"

"Yes. I've never been married and never had children."

He looked up from the yellow legal pad where he was scribbling notes. "Taking on three boys, that's quite an undertaking."

"Yes, it is, and I also run my own business. I'm a beautician."

"But you took them in?"

Cassie nodded. "I couldn't just abandon them to the system. They're good kids. I love them, and I want to give them a good life."

"Did you contact the authorities?"

"No. At first I just assumed Raymond would be back for them—that I was just watching the boys temporarily. I kept hoping Raymond would go back to rehab and get the help he needs. But it's been over a year."

"Has he been in contact with the children?"

"At first he called every few days, then once a week and then every few months. The last time he called, he didn't ask to speak with them, and he doesn't want them to see him."

She fell silent, fear making her stomach clench again as she recalled their last conversation.

"He told you that?"

"Yes. I offered to bring them to see him and he refused. My mother left me with my aunt and uncle when I was nine. They loved me, and they gave me the home that my mother couldn't provide. I want to do the same for the boys." She looked into the attorney's eyes. "Could I lose them?"

Mark leaned back in his chair, crossing one leg over the other. "It's true that the courts do try to keep the children with biological parents whenever possible. But given the situation you've described, I think it's doubtful they'd give the children back to him unless he proves he can provide a safe environment for them, especially since you've taken good care of them.

"You will be investigated, and they'll want to see that you're providing a stable home for the children. Your cousin left them with your aunt, but he knows they're with you, correct?"

"Yes."

Mark nodded, then asked, "Are you dating?"

"Griffin and I are seeing each other."

Again, Mark nodded. "Are you living together?"

"No. We only started dating recently. I think it's too early to say exactly where we're headed."

Mark studied her, flipping his pen from finger to finger. Finally, he said, "Judges like to see custodians in a committed relationship."

They discussed several other matters before Cassie left. She arrived at the bowling alley a little before four. The boys were bowling with Kevin. Emma and Aunt Luella sat at a table in the far corner, while Annie played on a blanket on the floor.

Cassie joined them.

"So, what happened?" Emma asked without waiting for her to sit down.

Cassie glanced at the bowling lanes to make sure the boys were occupied. She didn't want them to overhear their conversation. When she saw they were busy, she leaned back in her chair told them about meeting with the attorney.

"So what's next?" Aunt Luella asked.

"He said after he files papers, they will send out a caseworker, which means someone will come out to see where the boys live, talk to all of us, and make sure that I'm qualified to take care of them."

Aunt Luella puffed up with indignation. "Of course you are. There's no one better to take care of them."

Emma squeezed her hand. "You're great with them." "Thank you both." Cassie relished Emma and her aunt's encouragement. It strengthened her resolve to be the best parent she could be for the boys. They had been there to help her from the beginning, and she wouldn't have made it without their love and support.

"The lawyer's also going to contact Raymond and see if we can work out an agreement without having to go through the courts."

"If that boy was smart, he'd give you custody," Aunt Luella said.

Cassie silently agreed, but at the same time it hurt to think of the boys being permanently separated from their father.

"I want Raymond to stay in contact with them," Cassie said.

Her aunt picked up Annie and bounced her on her knee. "I believe he's doing what he thinks is best for them."

"Sometimes love means letting go," Emma said.

Annie began to fuss. Emma took the baby from her aunt and settled her in to nurse.

If only Raymond could have leaned on them when Maria died. Cassie knew with absolute certainty that she needed her family. They were her rock, and without them she'd never have made it through this last year. But time and again the one person she'd turned to was Griffin. He'd been there whenever she needed him. She didn't know how it happened, but sometime in the last year she'd fallen for him, and it would most certainly lead to heartbreak because even if Griffin felt the same way, he'd never let himself love again.

11

After dropping the boys at school on Monday morning, Cassie picked up some much needed groceries, then stopped at Death Wish, Betsy McGuire's drive-through coffee stand for a cup of her high octane brew before heading home. She put the groceries away, then sat at the kitchen table to read another letter from her mother.

Cassie:

I have so many regrets, most of them center around you. I loved you so much, but I was always torn between my love for you and my career. I wanted both, but I always chose it over you. The first time I left you with Aunt Luella and Uncle Albert, I was certain this was my big break that would get us out of the shabby apartment we were in. This was the band I'd played for before I got pregnant with you, and they'd signed with a music label after I left them.

I performed once on that trip, then they cut me from the band. I came back and went on a drinking binge, trying to drown my disappointment, then pulled myself together and picked you up. Aunt Luella and Uncle Albert tried to convince me to say in Hope's Crossing, but I refused. I was convinced my big break was out there waiting for me, and it wouldn't happen in a small town, so I loaded you up and drove back to Chicago.

Fragmented memories of that time swirled in Cassie's head. How she'd rushed into her mother's arms, and she'd swung her high into the air, then she'd been inconsolable when they left Hope's Crossing.

"Why couldn't we have stayed in Hope's Crossing, Mom?"

She knew the answer and intellectually understood that in order for her mother to have a shot at her career she had to be in Chicago, but Cassie still resented that she chose her career over her daughter.

Her phone buzzed. A text from Griffin.

Lunch today, just the two of us?

Where?

Your place?

She glanced at the stack of dirty dishes in the sink, the pile of laundry waiting to be washed and the floor covered in a layer of cereal from breakfast this morning.

Disaster zone here. Somewhere else?

I prefer messy.

He really did seem to thrive on it.

No complaints. You were warned.

Be there in twenty minutes.

Twenty minutes! She hadn't even showered. She raced to the bathroom and turned on the water while she brushed her teeth. Steam filled the bathroom as she stripped off her clothes and climbed into the shower.

GRIFFIN PARKED in Cassie's driveway, grabbed the flowers he'd picked up at the florist, and went inside. "Cassie?"

"In the kitchen."

He followed the scent of burned bread.

She had her back to him, stirring the pot on the stove, her hair in a messy ponytail just the way he liked. Soft music played from her phone.

He came up behind her and placed the flowers in front of her.

She buried her nose in them and inhaled. "Oh, I love daisies."

He wrapped a hand around her waist and nuzzled her neck, feeling her pulse jump. He smiled, pleased by her reaction.

Griffin swayed to the music and pressed his hips against hers.

"Hope you're hungry," Cassie said.

"Ravenous, but not for food."

She turned, looping her arms around his neck.

"I've wanted to be alone with you for the longest time," he said.

A provocative twinkle flared in her eyes. "Is that a fact?"

"It is."

"Well, you've got me alone, what do you intend to do with me, Dr. Valentine?"

He brushed his fingertips along the inside of her arm, and he felt her breath quicken.

A slow, sweet ballad played, and he swayed with her across the room, all too aware of her body pressed against his. He cupped her face, then pressed a soft kiss against her lips. She sighed, the sound filled with a need that a kiss alone couldn't complete.

"Griffin."

"Yes?"

"Make love to me."

CASSIE COLLAPSED BACK onto the bed after she and Griffin made love a second time. Her breath in short gasps and her heart galloping at the speed of light. Oh my, but the man knew exactly where to touch her.

He rolled to face her, a sheen of sweat glistening his forehead. "That was—"

"Amazing," Cassie finished for him.

His smile lit up his face, and her heart thudded when his finger traced over her lips. "I could do that again."

"Me, too."

His lips replaced his finger, and she would have given anything for more than a kiss, but they both had places to be. He released her and sat on the edge of the bed to gather his clothes.

She wrapped her arms around him and pressed her breasts to his back, her lips to his ear. "I wish we had more time."

He twisted so she fell into his lap, regret filling his eyes.. "And I would love to stay here with you if I didn't have patients waiting for me."

She trailed a finger down his chest. "A pity."

He captured her hand and kissed it before settling her back against the pillows. "We will find more than a few stolen hours together."

"Ha! Good luck with that." Between their work schedules and the boys, it would be difficult to find time alone.

As he buttoned his shirt, he glanced over his shoulder at her. "Challenge accepted."

His words sent her imagination into overdrive. When Griffin Valentine took a dare he kept it, and the idea of a repeat of this afternoon sounded like a slice of heaven.

She gave him a saucy wink. "I'm holding you to that."

He drew her into his arms and kissed her until she wanted to drag him back to bed for another round of lovemaking.

"A little something to remember me by."

"Oh my." She pulled on her clothes and trailed after him on shaky legs as he left the bedroom. Cassie made him a peanut butter and jelly sandwich to eat on the way back to work then invited him to dinner.

"Only if you'll let me cook."

She raised up on tiptoe and whispered, "How could I refuse you anything?" Her voice intimated a whole lot more than food.

He pulled her tightly against him. "You're a wicked woman," he murmured against her lips, then released her.

"You're just now figuring that out?"

His laughter boomed behind him as he walked out the door.

Cassie left minutes later to pick up the boys up from school. She dropped Trevor and Jeff at the Beauty Bowl before heading to Miss Minnie's School of Music where Tyler started trumpet lessons today. The poor kid was so excited he'd given himself a stomachache.

She squeezed his hand to reassure him, and he clung to her as they walked inside. She filled out the paperwork that the receptionist gave her. As they waited for class to begin, Tyler asked, "Cassie, what if I suck at this?"

She understood his fear, understood that gut-wrenching terror of attempting something new. "What if you do? What's the worst that could happen? You goof up. Big deal. You just keep practicing until you get better."

"But people might make fun of me."

"They might, but what if it turns out this is something you love? Would you want to miss out on that because you were scared you'd fail?"

Tyler considered her comment, then seemed to relax.

A few minutes later they met his teacher, and Cassie felt much better after talking with him. The man was kind, enthusiastic, and he believed anyone could learn to play the trumpet if that's what they wanted to. What more could she ask from a teacher?

WITH THE PLAYOFFS OVER and a week away from Halloween, it was time to close up the Cornhusker stadium for the season. Griffin cleared his appointments for Thursday to help Sam.

They finished mid-morning, and Griffin headed for home, sensing a hint of snow in the air. The nights had grown considerably cooler and had even dropped into the thirties. Farmers were rushing to get the last of their crops in.

Griffin finished his chores, then headed to the Beauty Bowl for a late lunch and to pick up the boys after they got out of school to help him winterize Cassie's place.

The boys were less than enthusiastic about his idea, but with the promise of pizza and a movie, especially on a school night, their attitude did a complete makeover.

He stuck his head in the beauty salon to tell Cassie they were leaving and wished he'd texted her instead. It was packed with customers, mostly the nosy, chatty ones including Becky Sue Walker.

He caught Cassie's eye in the mirror and motioned that he needed a private moment.

"Hold on just a second, Marlene. I'll be right back."

All eyes followed Cassie out of the shop where Griffin waited.

"What are you doing here?" she asked.

"I wanted you to know I'm taking the boys with me to do some yard work."

"Yard work? They agreed to that?"

"I was persuasive."

She leaned back against the glass wall, folding her arms over her chest. "And just what did you bribe them with?"

Griffin leaned in closer, catching a hint of lavender and whatever chemical she'd put on Marlene's hair. "Who says I bribed them?"

She smiled, the brilliance of it lighting her face. "I did."

"Dinner and a movie. Want to join us?"

"On a school night. I'm not sure that's a good idea."

"They're helping get your place winterized."

Her resistance melted. "Well, I think I can definitely make an exception in that instance." Her eyes darkened with the promise of more afternoon delight. "I was hoping you were going to suggest some time for us—alone."

He wanted that, too. Their afternoon getaway three days earlier seemed like an eternity ago. Griffin pressed his lips to hers and heard a burst of chatter from inside the salon. "I'll see you after work. Don't be late. The movie starts at six-thirty."

EVEN FOR A WEEKNIGHT, the theater was crowded with children and adults. Cassie and Griffin sat in the loge section while the kids all sat in the front two rows, their necks craned as they watched the upcoming previews. Cassie remembered doing the same thing when she was a kid.

Griffin whispered, "Look at Trevor." He pointed to the second row, where he sat next to Katy Miller.

She grew nostalgic as she recalled her first crush back in eighth grade. She and Ricky Singleton had come to the movies with Sam and his brother, Ryan, Emma, Bella, and Griffin. They'd all sat in the front row just like the kids were doing now, and Ricky had inched out Griffin to sit next to her.

She cast a glance at Griffin, wondering about his motives back then.

Trevor leaned closer to Katy, and Cassie experienced a moment of trepidation. She had a soon-to-be teenager on her hands, and she didn't have a clue how she would handle that.

Griffin squeezed her hand, nodding toward Trevor. "Relax and enjoy the movie. Trevor and Katy are just sitting there. Nothing else is going on."

"Maybe not now, but that can change in a year or two."

"And it probably won't be Katy by then. It will be another girl. Just like you and Ricky didn't last."

She drew back in surprise. "You remember that?"

Griffin gave her a quick kiss. "Of course I do. I was so jealous I wanted to rip you two apart, but you only had eyes for Ricky." Griffin's eyes glittered in the light of the screen. "I guess I've always wanted to be more than just your friend."

"Shush." Lord Mumford shinned a flashlight on them. "The movie is about to begin."

Cassie pressed her lips together to restrain a smile. She and Griffin both mumbled their apologies and settled back to watch the movie, but Cassie's heart was full to brimming with the knowledge Griffin had wanted her all those years ago.

12

Cassie dropped the kids at school the next morning, then went to the salon. The morning flew by and it was lunch time before she knew it. She and Griffin had planned a picnic at the park across the street from his office—burgers from the Beauty Bowl.

Cassie arrived first, found a table, and spread out a beach towel she'd brought from her car, then texted Griffin.

Food's getting cold.

Be there in five.

She sent him an emoji heart.

Cassie leaned back against the table and tipped her face to the sky absorbing the sun's warmth. A perfect fall day, brisk, but not too cold for a picnic.

A shadow fell over her face and her eyes fluttered open to find Griffin standing over her. He braced his hands on the table and leaned in to kiss her. Not a gentle welcoming kiss, but one that promised wild, passionate sex. He pulled back, and his gaze flickered over her, leaving her wanting for so much more.

"Don't look at me like that." It came out as an order, but the way his eyes swept over her it felt more like a plea.

"Maybe we should eat our lunch before it gets cold," she suggested.

He sat down beside her. "The only thing I'm hungry for is you."

She smiled at him as she handed him a burger. "We picked the wrong place for that."

"Next time we'll do something different."

She unwrapped her burger, then said, "About next time."

He set his burger down. "What about it?"

"I want a relationship that's more than some stolen afternoons when the kids aren't around. I'm not that kind of woman."

He scrubbed a hand over his face. "No you're not, and I'm sorry if you felt I was treating you that way. If Mom were here she'd be lecturing me on how to treat a woman I care about."

"So, you think of me as more than a friend you have sex with?"

Griffin shook his head. "I'm sorry. I'm really not good at this." He turned so he straddled the bench and looked her in the eye. "I have feelings for you that go beyond friendship. I always have, but I only just recently realized it. They're growing every day. I don't know how deep they go, and honestly it scares me. My relationships have all ended poorly because I'm too much like my father. Career before family was his motto."

Cassie trailed her fingers across his chiseled jaw. "I disagree. From the day you returned to Hope's Crossing you have made my needs a priority, however, there are times I feel shut out, especially when it comes to sharing about yourself. I need intimacy, Griffin, and it's something I never had in my past relationships. I want marriage, children and happily-ever-after, but what I really want is that deep connection with the man I'm involved with, and I won't settle for anything less."

He was silent a long moment, then said, "I'll make every effort to give you that, Cass."

It wasn't exactly what she'd hoped for, but it was a start. "There's a part of me that wants you to swear that you won't hurt me, that you'll always be there for me and the boys. But life is about taking risks, and if I don't take a chance on us and see where this goes, I'll regret it."

She laid a hand on his chest. "I want to tell the boys we're in a serious relationship. Are you on board with that?"

His expression went from trepidation to joy. "Absolutely. And I promise I will do everything in my power to make you happy."

"What do you say we tell them tonight?"

His smile filled her with happiness. "It's a date."

She wiggled her eyebrows. "Be sure and bring a change of clothes."

His eyes held hers. "Are you sure?"

"Positive."

A growl rumbled through him as he took her in his arms and kissed her, confirming their relationship had taken a whole new direction.

GRIFFIN WAS at the house when she got home from work. He had dinner cooking, and he was helping the boys with their homework. The man might not share his inner most feelings with her, but he sure knew how to woo a woman.

He looked up from Tyler's homework when she entered the kitchen and her belly tightened when she spotted his overnight bag in the corner. She leaned in to press her lips to his. Before she could pull back, his arms came around her and he deepened the kiss, then released her, her face still in inches from his. "That's a proper welcome home kiss."

She ignored Tyler's snicker and spoke to Griffin. "I'll keep that in mind." She turned away and headed for the bedroom to change out of her work clothes, snagging Griffin's bag on the way, Jeff's sing/songy voice following her down the hall.

"Griffin and Cassie sittin' in a tree."

Relationships were not simple with children in the mix.

CASSIE CLEARED the table after dinner.

"I'm going to play a video game," Jeff said, hopping out of his chair.

"Wait, Griffin and I have something we need to discuss with you guys."

"Now," Jeff whined.

"Yes."

Jeff plopped back down in his chair and folded his arms over his chest, thrusting out his jaw.

Cassie pursed her lips to hide the smile threatening and sat beside Griffin. His hand covered hers, warm and reassuring. "As you guys are aware, Griffin and I have been dating."

Jeff rolled his eyes, clearly unimpressed, but Cassie didn't let his attitude deter her. "We care about each other, so we want to see more of each other than just dinner once in a while, so Griffin will be staying overnight here. He may be picking you guys up, too, and helping me take care of you."

"Does that mean he's getting our bedroom?" Jeff demanded.

Tyler rolled his eyes. "No dummy. He's going to stay in Cassie's room."

Jeff's eyes widened. "Like Emma and Sam?"

Cassie hesitated, not sure how to answer, and Griffin stepped in. "Yes, like that."

Jeff took the information in stride. "Okay, can I go play video games now?"

"You don't have any questions?"

Jeff shook his head, and Cassie waved him off. "What about you two?" she asked Tyler and Trevor.

Trevor shrugged. "I'm okay with it."

She looked at Tyler. "What about you?"

He scowled at her. "It's not like I have any say. You took his bag to the bedroom so you've already decided."

Cassie laid her hand over his. "It's true, we did make our decision, but we want to hear your concerns."

Tyler's eyes turned bleak. "Okay. When you and Griffin get married and have your own kids, what happens to us?"

Cassie's heart twisted. She understood his fears, and would have felt the same way. "No matter what happens between Griffin and me, this is your home and nothing, *nothing* will ever change that."

She gathered Tyler into her arms and held him close. "I love you." She looked at Trevor. "All of you, and I'm not letting you go, *ever*."

"Even if Dad comes back?" Trevor asked.

Cassie swallowed back the lump in her throat. "Yes."

Griffin's arm came around her and he reiterated what she'd said. "This is your home. No matter what, but I'd very much like to be a part of it. Are you guys okay with that?"

Trevor and Tyler both nodded.

He held up his hand and they high-fived him.

"Griffin, do you have time to play catch with me before it gets dark?" Trevor asked, his voice hesitant as if he'd been rejected all too frequently in his young life.

"Sure. Get my glove out of the backseat of my truck while I help Cassie clean up."

Cassie glanced out the window as the sun angled low in the sky. She gave him a nudge. "Go while you've still got light. Tyler and I can manage, right?"

He nodded against her chest, still curled in her lap.

Griffin squeezed her shoulder, then followed Trevor out the front door. If she was going to take a chance, she couldn't have picked a better man.

Tyler tilted his head back to look her in the eyes. "You really like him, don't you?"

She pressed a kiss to the top of his head. "Yes."

GRIFFIN FOLLOWED Cassie to her bedroom after they got the boys to bed, his hand lightly riding the small of her back. Just that simple touch and he wanted to take her right here in the hallway. He didn't, but the instant the bedroom door closed, he pulled her close and kissed until they were both breathing heavy.

"I've wanted to do that all night," he said.

Cassie released a breathless laugh. "I've wanted to do a whole lot more than that."

Griffin pressed her back against the door, his body snug against hers. "Really. What did you have in mind?"

She fingered the button on his shirt. "That I wanted to drag you to the bedroom, strip off your clothes, and—"

He gulped in a breath. "And what?"

A provocative smile played on her lips as she slipped under his arm and moved toward the bathroom. Lifting her shirt, she tossed it on the floor. "I'm thinking we could both use a good scrubbing. Want to join me in the shower?"

She shimmied out of jeans and stepped into the bathroom. A moment later, he heard the water come on.

He started to undress, but Cassie's voice stopped him. "Wait. I want to help."

She leaned against the bathroom doorway completely naked, and the blood surged to his groin.

She crooked a finger at him. "Come here big boy."

With those simple words, he'd do anything she asked. He crossed over to her and her hands slipped under his shirt. He was on fire with need and ready to take her right here against the wall.

She lifted his shirt and tossed it aside, then her hands slipped below his waistband and that fire turned into a raging inferno. He clasped her wrists above her head and pinned her against the wall, then kissed her.

Steam swirled around them as the kiss deepened.

When he finally pulled back, Cassie said, "You have too many clothes on."

He grinned at her. "Not for long."

GRIFFIN AWOKE TO A "YIPPEE" early the next morning. Footsteps thudded outside the bedroom door. Griffin quickly pulled on his boxers and met them at the door.

Jeff gaped up at him. "How come you're in your underwear?" he asked with the innocent guile only a nine-year-old could express.

"Because it's not comfortable to sleep in my jeans."

"Oh." He brightened, accepting Griffin's explanation without question. "Guess what?"

"What?"

"There's no school today."

"How come?"

"We're snowed in. A blizzard."

Jeff grabbed Griffin's hand and dragged him to his bedroom window across the hall. Sure enough there was a full out blizzard in progress. His gut twisted. Snow made everything beautiful, but at the same time treacherous.

Griffin closed his eyes, when a sudden memory of his son flashed in his mind—that sweet smile and trusting eyes, gone in an instant.

Pushing the memories aside, he focused on the here and now. First things first, he would close the office. "You're right, we are snowed in."

The boys shouted again, and Griffin shushed them. "Cassie is still sleeping, and I'm going back to bed. You guys either do the same or play quietly until we wake up and make breakfast. Okay?"

They nodded and elbowed each other as the muffled thud of their footsteps against the carpet echoed all the way to the living room. Griffin shook his head and figured he'd be lucky if he went back to sleep. He texted his receptionist to cancel all their appointments for the day, then climbed into bed, wrapped his arms around Cassie, and immediately fell back to sleep.

FAINT LIGHT FILTERED through the curtains when Cassie woke, and something tickled her nose. She brushed it away, and it immediately came back, along with a giggle. She cracked open an eye to find Jeff and Tyler holding a feather and preparing to tickle Griffin with it next.

"I wouldn't—"

Before she could finish the sentence, Griffin swooped up, grabbed each boy around the waist and pulled them onto the bed between them. It was a good thing she'd put on her nightgown earlier.

Contentment filled her as she watched Griffin with the boys. What she'd thought would be an awkward transition to having him stay overnight, he made seamless, and it touched her deeply how well he dealt with the kids.

"Why are you two waking us up?" Griffin demanded, his voice stern with mock annoyance, but his eyes alight with teasing laughter.

"We're hungry," they said.

"Hungry! How can you two be hungry?" Griffin demanded.

Jeff shrugged. "We're kids. We're always hungry."

That produced a deep chuckle. "So, what do you want us to do about it?"

Tyler bounced on his knees. "Make pancakes."

They never got tired of pancakes. How could they want the same food day-after-day, Cassie wondered.

"Why don't you make them?" Griffin asked.

Jeff gave him a wide-eyed look. "We're kids. That's what moms do."

Griffin cast a dubious glance at the boys, then her. "Is that right, Mom?"

Mom? Were they talking about her? She wasn't a mom. Moms made pancakes that weren't raw in the middle.

Griffin must have seen the lack of confidence in her eyes because he squeezed her hand in reassurance. "Since it's a snow day and we can't go anywhere, I think it's a good day to teach you guys how to make pancakes."

And maybe Cassie could pick up some pointers, too.

"We're kids. You're supposed to make 'em, not us," Tyler said.

"How do you suppose moms and dads learn to make pancakes?" Griffin asked.

Jeff shrugged. "I dunno."

"Their moms and dads taught them."

"So, are you going to teach us?" Trevor asked from the doorway.

He looked so small and vulnerable, standing there all by himself. Cassie held out a free arm, and he came to her. She hugged him, and he ducked his head in embarrassment.

Griffin reached over and rubbed the side of his head.

"Hey." He pulled back, gleeful revenge in his eyes as he reached out to rub his knuckles across Griffin's scalp.

Griffin ducked out of reach. "Okay, everybody out while we get dressed, then I'll teach you how to make pancakes."

"I thought Cassie was going to teach us."

"We are all treating Cassie to the morning off. Now scram. And close the door," Griffin ordered.

Without a word they scattered, slamming the door behind them. Griffin drew her into his arms. "Now that I've got you to myself, how about a little pre-breakfast snack."

A giggle sounded from outside the door, followed by a whispered, "Shush, they're gonna kiss."

Cassie laughed. "I think that's going to have to wait since we have an audience right outside the door."

Griffin rolled her underneath him. "At least give me a good morning kiss before I make you breakfast."

Cassie complied and gave a whole lot more than he'd asked for.

13

As promised, Griffin taught the boys how to make pancakes. Before they finished, flour covered every inch of the counter and the boys. Griffin also showed them that cooking meant cleaning up after yourself. When they were done, the kitchen was spotless, and he even hustled the boys to the bathroom.

While they worked, Cassie called her clients and cancelled her appointments for the day.

She looked out the window, watching the snow drift from the sky. Rarely, did they have more than a dusting of snow in late-October, but this was a full-blown winter storm. At the rate it was falling, they might not get out tomorrow either.

After the boys got dressed and brushed their teeth, Griffin put them to work. He bundled them up and had them shovel the sidewalk while he started the snow blower and cleared the driveway.

An hour later, they were all back inside, a pile of wet clothing at the door. Cassie had hot chocolate ready, and they all settled in to watch a movie.

Griffin pulled her aside. "So, do I get a reward for all my hard work this morning?"

Cassie tapped her finger against her chin and pretended to think. "The satisfaction of a job well done."

"Un-uh."

"The satisfaction of helping out a friend in need?"

He leaned closer to her so that the warmth of his breath whispered over her skin. "Nope."

"Sorry, can't help you then."

Griffin leaned in closer and growled, "Maybe I'll just take my reward."

"Maybe you should."

And he did. He drew her out of sight of the boys and kissed her until her her heart threatened to thump right out of her chest. Voices drifted from the living room, pulling Cassie from her romantic musings.

"Hey, that's mine."

"Is not."

"Is too."

"Will you guys knock it off? I can't hear the movie."

Cassie bumped her forehead against Griffin's chest and groaned. "And so it begins."

Griffin's laugh rumbled in his chest. "My brothers and I did this all the time, and for the most part, we worked it out. You've got to let them do the same."

Easier said than done. "They could get hurt, not to mention their fighting drives me crazy."

"I didn't say let them beat each other senseless, but ignore the minor bickering."

Cassie released a pent up breath. She knew he was right, but it was damned easy to give advice—much harder to put into practice. "You're right. I just worry I'm going to mess up."

Another laugh. "Of course you will. No one ever gets it just right."

She shoved his shoulder. "Thanks a lot."

"Would you rather I lie?"

"Maybe a little."

He hugged her close. "If we were alone, I'd show you just how perfect you are."

She sighed, wishing for that, but knowing it wasn't likely.

Just then they heard bells tingling. "What's that?" Cassie asked.

Griffin looked as bewildered as her. They went to the living room window and saw two sleighs pulling up to the house. Sam, Emma holding Annie, and Kevin sat in one, and Aunt Luella and Sam's dad, Joe, Matt and Bella drove another. Griffin ushered them inside, and Cassie got a fresh pot of coffee going.

"What are you doing out in this weather?" she asked her aunt.

"Sam and Joe thought it would be fun to hitch up the sleighs and go for a ride. They thought you and the kids would like to join us."

A whoop sounded from the family room, where the boys had apparently just been notified about the impending sleigh ride. Before Cassie could tell them to get their gear on, Griffin beat her to it.

Her aunt wore that matchmaker's knowing look. "That man's a keeper."

Cassie wagged a finger at her. "Don't start."

"What?" Her innocent expression might have been comical if not for the calculating gleam in her eyes. "So, when exactly did Griffin get here?"

Trevor picked that exact moment to enter the kitchen. "Griffin came to dinner last night and he was here when we woke up."

Her aunt's penciled brows almost disappeared into her hairline. "Is that a fact?"

"Griffin's always here when we need him," Trevor continued.

A keeper, her aunt mouthed.

Cassie nudged Trevor toward his bedroom. "Go get your snow gear on so we can go for a ride."

Trevor retreated, but she didn't miss the grin that engulfed his face. He might just have a touch of Aunt Luella's matchmaking gene. God help her if there were two in the family.

～

TEN MINUTES LATER, they set off. The snow continued to fall, but not as heavily as it had earlier. It never ceased to amaze Griffin how snow changed everything. Nothing looked the same, and the pristine white was a sight to behold. Annie played peekaboo with him over Emma's shoulder. Bittersweet memories assaulted him as he remembered how Bobby had loved the snow from the time he was Annie's age. How different Griffin's life would have been if his son had lived. He'd probably still be living in Chicago, working long hours and putting his career first. He missed his son deeply, and he wished Bobby were here with him right now so he could be a different father.

Annie held her arms out to him, and he took her from Emma. She smacked his cheeks with tiny gloved hands and laughed then tilted her face to the sky and opened her mouth.

Cassie chucked Annie under the chin, and her laughter sent warmth coursing through him that no amount of hot coffee could accomplish. "Just like your mama. Love the snow."

Annie giggled and squirmed in his arms.

Sam hit a bump and drew another delighted laugh from his daughter.

They headed west toward town so that Luella could check on the Beauty Bowl, and Annie snuggled against Griffin's chest, her pudgy arms wrapped around his neck. Her breathing slowed and evened out, and he realized she'd fallen asleep. What would it be like if he and Cassie had a baby?

He looked at Cassie and found her staring at Annie with something akin to longing in her eyes.

She met his gaze, and the warmth there kindled a yearning for more than sex. She was the woman he could start over with, build a new life with. Sure it came with children, but that didn't mean they couldn't add one or two more. One question that haunted him. Was he a changed man? Would he be there for Cassie when she needed him?

Annie stirred, and wide blue eyes fluttered open, full of innocence and trust. Her mouth began working, and within a minute or two her head craned around as she searched for Emma. When she saw her mother, she reached out to her. Griffin handed her back and felt an immediate loss.

"It's hard to let her go, isn't it?" Cassie asked.

He nodded, his emotions too raw to speak.

Cassie studied him, the snow blurring his vision of her.

Griffin sensed there was a dual meaning behind her words and a moment later he was certain when she asked, "Because it reminds you of Bobby?"

Griffin nodded but didn't elaborate. "I wish I deserved a second chance."

She brushed a gloved hand across his cheek. "You deserve it all. You were the best father you knew how to be."

If only that were true. The fact was he'd failed his son, but there was nothing he could do to change that. He had to find a way to live with it, and he was determined to try because he'd found the one woman who was perfect for him in every way.

THEY DROVE THROUGH TOWN, the street lights aglow with a yellow haze that made it look like early evening instead of midday. Shovels were removed from the sleighs, and the men took turns clearing a path into the Beauty Bowl while the kids built snowmen in the parking lot. More neighborhood kids joined in, and soon there was a whole row of snowmen in progress.

A bark, then a blur of motion as Rookie raced down the row of snowmen to join in the melee. A moment later, Chet materialized.

Luella let out a loud whoop, and the clatter of childish voices fell silent. "This is some fine work you've done to help clear the snow, so I declare we have a snowman judging contest. As soon as the walk is cleared to the Beauty Bowl, I'll bring out items for you to add to your snowmen or snowwomen as the case may be."

The kids jumped up and down and cheered, then went back to fine-tune their creations.

Emma whispered to Cassie, "Aunt Luella always comes up with

the best projects. I'm going to have to take notes. Look at how much snow she's gotten removed for free and without complaint."

Cassie laughed. "She is devious that way."

Luella waved Chet over. "And Coach Cooper is going to be one of the judges."

Her father's eyes widened with surprise. He said something to her aunt she couldn't hear then grinned and agreed to participate.

The cowbell clanked, indicating the path was clear. Cassie started to follow her aunt inside, but Chet drew her aside before she could.

"I'm sorry. I didn't intend to intrude on your family gathering. I was just taking Rookie for a walk, and he spotted the kids."

Cassie was torn. Part of her wanted to hold him at arm's length and protect her heart, but longing pulled at her with equal strength. She'd watched him from afar growing up, and finally, when she'd given up hope of ever getting to know him, he walked into her life.

The loneliness lurking in his eyes made her decision. "It's okay. You're welcome to join in, and the kids will love having you judge their snowmen."

"Thank you. I—"

Rookie barked and leaped at a snowball Tyler threw in the air, interrupting what he'd been about to say.

Cassie went inside to help her aunt. Minutes later they carried out the recycling bin, and the kids immediately began searching through it. Her aunt also brought out carrots, gummy worms, sour strips, and candy corn.

The kids began decorating the snowmen and snacking on candy. When it looked like most of them had finished Aunt Luella called out, "Ten minutes left.".

The kids rushed around making finishing touches on their creations.

"Time's up," Aunt Luella declared. "Okay judges, find us a winner for each category."

Her aunt had conned Joe, Sam, and Griffin into helping Chet judge by promising them hot coffee and a slice of apple pie for their efforts. They'd all readily agreed.

Tyler and his friend, Bryan, won for the most creative with sticks for arms and plastic water bottles for mittens, black bottle caps for eyes, and red licorice for the mouth.

Trevor and Katy Miller had paired up, and they won the most fashionable. Their snowwoman sported a shawl, a pair of hoop earrings, and false eyelashes Katy had run home to borrow from her sister. Jeff and Kevin won with the most edible snowman—the face made of candy, bananas for arms, and Oreo cookies covered the head for a hat. The winners each received blue ribbons that Luella always kept on hand, then everyone had pie and ice cream.

Chet had walked Rookie to town from the house he'd rented down the street from Cassie. When Sam had offered him a ride home on the sleigh, he'd accepted. Rookie immediately laid down at Cassie's feet, not moving the entire ride. The kids were tired and ready for dinner by the time they got home, which to Cassie's surprise Griffin had all planned out. He'd gotten the meat out to thaw before they'd left, and in no time, he had a huge pot of spaghetti ready. It was an early dinner so that everyone could get home before the next storm rolled in, which forecasters predicted would dump even more snow.

Chet came up beside her. "Do you have a couple of towels I can dry Rookie with?"

"Sure. I'll be right back." She returned with the towels, and they worked together to dry him. Rookie apparently loved it as he pressed closer, urging her to rub harder.

"He's taken a real shine to you."

Cassie dried his neck, then jumped back when he shook.

Laughing, she said, "From what I've seen, he loves everyone."

Chet rubbed down his back. "He does, but he's particularly smitten with you."

Cassie kneeled down and rubbed Rookie's ear but didn't admit except to herself that she'd taken a shine to him, too, because Chet would eventually return to his home in Idaho. It hurt to think about either of them leaving, so she ignored the thought and pushed to her feet. She found herself face-to-face with Chet.

"Are you sure I'm not intruding being here?" he asked.

"No, you're not." Cassie was surprised she meant it. She was actually happy he'd come. "It's freezing out here. Let's go inside and have some of Griffin's spaghetti."

Rookie shook then barked his agreement.

They both laughed, and Rookie led the way inside.

CASSIE AND BELLA sat at the table and sipped tea while Emma changed Annie's diaper.

Bella grimaced and rubbed her extended belly.

"Are you okay?" Cassie asked.

"Yes, just more Braxton Hicks contractions. I am so ready for this baby to get here. My feet are swollen, my bellybutton has gone from an innie to an outie, and I can't bend over to put on my shoes."

Cassie had heard the same complaints from Emma just before she went into labor with Annie, but she didn't miss the anxiousness in Bella's voice. Her cousin was scared this baby would end up like her first.

Cassie hugged her close, and whispered, "Everything is going to be fine."

Bella trembled in her arms. "Matt keeps telling me the same thing, but I just keep remembering the hushed silence after I delivered Tessa." She shuddered. "I don't know what I'd do if it happened again."

Cassie pulled back and looked her directly in the eye. "The baby is still moving, isn't she?"

"Yes."

"And Tessa stopped moving a week or two before you went into labor, didn't she?"

Bella gave a hesitant nod.

"Has Griffin or your specialist indicated they've seen a problem?"

"No."

Cassie squeezed her hand. "After what you've been through, don't you think if they suspected something was wrong they would take action and order tests to be on the safe side?"

The tension slowly eased from Bella's face. "Yes, they promised me they would."

"Griffin is a man of his word."

"He is."

"I'm not trying to make light of your fears, but you've done everything you possibly can to ensure her safety, so focus on holding her in your arms."

Bella blinked back tears. "Thank you."

Cassie gave her hand another squeeze. "Everything is going to be fine."

Emma came back, and Bella took Annie and hugged her close. The best medicine ever, in Cassie's opinion.

Kevin materialized at Emma's side and tugged on her shirt. "Can Jeff come home with us so I have someone to play with?"

"What did your dad say?" she asked.

"He said it was fine with him," Kevin said with perfect innocence, but Cassie sensed that Emma was being played.

"Let me talk to him, then I'll discuss it with Cassie." Emma went over to confer with Sam while Kevin bounced on the balls of his feet, anxiously awaiting the outcome.

Cassie and Bella grinned when Sam's gaze moved to his son. The kid dug his toe into the carpet and tensed under his father's perusal. When Sam finally nodded and smiled, Kevin let out a whoop, and he and Jeff raced down the hall to Jeff's bedroom without waiting for Cassie's agreement.

"Are you sure this isn't too much?" Cassie asked Emma when she came back over. "You do know there is more snow predicted. You could have him an extra day."

"We'll be fine," Emma assured her. "It might even be better because Kevin will have someone to play with, and we can always hitch up the sleigh and bring him home if need be."

Trevor was deep in conversation with Luella before he turned to

Cassie. "Cassie, can me and Tyler go back to Aunt Luella's? She needs help shoveling snow. Then we can play with our friends."

A dull red crept up Trevor's neck. Cassie would bet going to Aunt Luella's had less to do with shoveling snow and more to do with seeing Katy.

Cassie looked at her aunt. "Is that all right with you?"

"It was my idea. I can't shovel those walks all by myself."

Why did Cassie get the impression that her aunt would have plenty of help between the boys and Joe Parker? She'd been seeing Luella and Joe together more frequently. If she didn't know better, she'd think something was going on between them.

"Okay, pack extra clothes in case you can't get home tomorrow."

The boys were already rushing off before she finished speaking.

Within minutes, she and Griffin were alone with an entire evening to themselves. While he pulled his truck into the garage, Cassie turned on the water in the enormous soaker tub and added bubble bath. While it filled, she lit candles, then peeled off her clothes and climbed into the tub, leaned back, and sighed.

14

G riffin's phone vibrated. He glanced at the text.
I'm in the tub. Want to join me?
More steamy sex. He was definitely in and responded with, *Hell ya.*

She sent an emoji of a volcano erupting and a smiley face winking.

He went inside through the garage and stripped off his coat, leaving a trail of clothing to the bedroom. Soft music came from the bathroom. He found Cassie just where he wanted her—in the bathtub filled with bubbles, candles flickering from the countertop, and her eyes closed.

He crawled in and scooted her forward to sit behind her.

Her breasts glistened in the flickering candlelight. He cupped one, and she sighed before twisting around to press her lips to his. Water sloshed over the side of the tub. "What took you so long?"

He pulled her on top of him, the warm water lapping over her back. "I'm meticulous with any job I take on, even if it's just parking the truck in the garage."

Cassie's fingers drifted down his chest and under the water. "Is that a fact?"

"It is."

She cupped him, and he took in a sharp inhale of breath.

A saucy light filled her eyes. "Prove it."

GRIFFIN'S PHONE buzzed shortly after midnight.

"Griffin, it's Matt. Bella's in labor. We were headed for the hospital, but we're stuck in the snow about a mile from Cassie's house." Matt lowered his voice. "She's panicking that we won't make it to the hospital in time."

"How long has she been in labor?"

"Less than thirty minutes."

"How far apart are the contractions?"

"A minute and a half."

There was no way they would make it to the hospital in time to deliver. "Stay there, and I'll come get you."

"Tell me everything is going to be all right."

"Everything is going to be okay. The best thing you can do is stay calm and keep reassuring Bella."

He ended the call and started pulling on his clothes.

"Where are you going?" Cassie murmured, her voice raspy with sleep.

"Bella's in labor, and they're stuck in the snow about a mile from here."

Cassie tossed back the covers and began yanking on her clothes.

"Where do you keep the flashlights?" he asked.

"Top shelf in the pantry."

Griffin had just found the flashlights when Cassie came out with a stack of blankets. "Is there anything else we need to bring?"

"This should be it for now. I'm hoping we can get her back to the house before she gives birth."

Cassie grabbed his arm. "She and the baby will be okay, won't they?"

"Everything is going to be fine." Griffin just prayed he was right. While it was unlikely she'd have another stillbirth, it did happen. But there was no way they could get an ambulance or

Life Flight to the couple in time, so he would have to deliver the baby.

Cassie pulled up the hood of her coat and followed him out to his truck. The wind blew snow into their path. Fortunately, it was dry, but brutally cold.

Griffin started the truck and slowly eased down the driveway and onto the road while Cassie called for an ambulance.

She ended the call. "They're not sure when it can get here."

Not surprising, given the weather. He inched along, the driving snow making it difficult to see. Fortunately, Matt was closer to Cassie's house than he realized.

Griffin turned the truck around so they were headed back toward Cassie's house, then parked the truck alongside Matt's SUV.

Griffin went to the passenger side and found Bella pale and in the middle of a contraction. When it passed, he asked Matt, "How long was this one?"

"A minute, and they're coming almost on top of each other."

"Help me get her into the truck."

Together they got her out of the car. Her moan echoed over the wind as they reached his truck. "Another contraction?"

"Yes," Bella hissed.

"We're going to help you into the truck. I know it's hard, but try to breathe through it," Griffin told her.

Bella nodded and focused on the contraction.

They got her buckled in, and Matt drove them back to the house while Griffin checked her vitals. "Good, strong heartbeat."

Bella breathed a sigh of relief.

Matt pulled into the garage, and Cassie went in ahead of them. Another contraction hit, stronger than the last one. Bella gripped the doorway until it passed.

They got her inside, and Griffin led her to the pellet stove where Cassie had put an air mattress and covered it with clean sheets.

Griffin focused on Bella.

Her teeth chattered. She looked up at Griffin, her eyes dark with worry. "Is my baby going to be okay?"

He took her blood pressure then listened to the baby's heart beat again. "Everything is normal. Bella, I have no reason to expect you're going to have problems with this delivery, and from the looks of it this baby is going to be here shortly."

She nodded, but she didn't look reassured. She probably wouldn't be until she held the baby in her arms.

Griffin found Cassie in the kitchen. "I need some towels, and I don't suppose you have any baby blankets?"

"I'll find something we can use." She started down the hall and stopped with Griffin's next words.

"I may need your help when the baby is coming."

Cassie nodded. He knew she didn't handle blood well, but he also knew she would suck it up and do what needed to be done for Bella and her baby.

MATT SQUEEZED BELLA'S HAND. "Just one more push and you'll be holding our baby in your arms."

"I can't. I'm too tired."

"You can do it." The strength in Matt's voice reenergized Cassie's cousin and Bella bore down.

The baby arrived with the next push, a beautiful, healthy baby girl with a loud, lusty cry that had Bella and Cassie in tears.

Cassie had never doubted Griffin's skill as a doctor, but with Bella's history she'd been concerned.

Matt tenderly brushed the damp tendrils of hair from Bella's forehead and pressed a kiss to her lips. "Thank you for our beautiful daughter."

Bella radiated pure bliss—something Cassie hadn't seen since before Shawn, her ex-husband broke her heart.

"Have you picked a name yet?"

Bella's eyes sparkled. "Madelyn Luella. We're naming her after Matt's mother and Aunt Luella."

"It's beautiful." Cassie leaned over and traced a finger over the baby's silky cheek. "Welcome to the world Maddie."

An hour later, she and Griffin slipped out of the room to make coffee and give the family some private time. Cassie glanced out the window. The snow continued to fall as the snowplows cleared the road. The ambulance arrived a little after eight and loaded up Bella, the baby, and Matt and drove them to the hospital.

Cassie and Griffin cleaned up, threw the sheets and towels into the washer, then fell into bed, sleeping through the morning.

Cassie's phone vibrated on the nightstand a little before noon. She glanced at it, and when she saw it was from Aunt Luella, she went into the next room to answer it so she wouldn't disturb Griffin.

"Hello."

"Oh, you are there. I was about to hang up."

"I'm here. We had a little excitement last night and didn't get to bed until after eight this morning."

"What happened?"

"Bella went into labor, and they got stuck on the way to the hospital. We brought them here, and they have a beautiful baby girl."

"Oh for land's sake, that is wonderful news. What did they name her?"

"Madelyn Luella."

There was a catch in her aunt's voice. "Oh my goodness."

"I'm sure you could call the hospital and talk to her."

There was a pause, then, "I'll do that as soon as I hang up."

"Why are you calling?"

"Oh, completely slipped my mind. Tyler's ready to come home."

Cassie looked out at the snow that continued to fall, but the road had been plowed and the ambulance had made it through, so she could, too. "Tell him I'll be there as soon as I can."

"Drive careful."

"I will."

Cassie went back to the bedroom and got dressed then left a note on the pillow for Griffin telling him where she'd gone. She turned to leave, and his hand clasped her wrist. She looked down to see one clearly exhausted, sleepy-eyed male staring up at her.

"Where are you going?"

"To Aunt Luella's. Tyler wants to come home."

"What's wrong?"

"Nothing. He's just ready to come home. I'm going to run in and get him. Go back to sleep."

Fury burned in his eyes. "You were going to drive in this weather without telling me?"

"I left you a note." She gestured to the paper beside him, confused by his reaction. Then she realized the colossal error she'd made. This was how he'd lost Bobby. A snowy day, a simple car ride, and a truck sliding out of control had resulted in tragedy. What had she been thinking?

"I knew you were tired. I didn't want to disturb you. I'm sorry I didn't think."

Griffin pushed to a sitting position and scrubbed a hand over his face. "Storms like this aren't something to fool around with."

They weren't, and she knew it, but she'd been focused on Tyler.

Griffin pulled her down beside him. "I'm sorry. I overreacted. It's just, after last night...Matt and Bella were so lucky. Something horrible could have happened to them."

It wasn't last night he was thinking about—it was memories of Bobby's accident.

She gripped Griffin's hand. "The roads have been plowed. I'll go slow."

His gaze held hers. "He wants to come home to his mom."

Cassie froze, suddenly realizing at some point that she'd become Tyler's mother—a mother to all three of them. When had she started thinking like a real parent? When had she started thinking of these boys as her own? Oh God, what would she do when Raymond came back for them? She'd be devastated and lost without them.

"I'm sorry, I was just thinking about Tyler."

The worry lines across Griffin's forehead smoothed out. "I know, but you can't leave me to worry and wonder with the weather like this. We go together." He tugged her into his arms. "We're a team. I care about you, Cass. I couldn't bear it if something happened to you or the boys."

She cupped his face and pressed her mouth to his, kissing him long and slow. "I never meant to worry you. I'm new at this relationship stuff, too. It's going to take some time to remember I have help."

His hand rested behind the back of her neck. Pressing her closer, he deepened the kiss. When he released her, he stroked her face. "We'll work it out. Let me get dressed, and we'll go get your boy."

She liked the sound of that. Her boy. Her children. Raymond had left them with her, and they'd become hers. Somehow she would have to find a way to convince him to let them stay here permanently.

CASSIE WOKE on Monday morning with Griffin's arms around her and her back pressed tightly against his chest. She tried to ease away without waking him, but every time she moved, his arms tightened around her. She stilled, waited a few minutes, then tried again. But each time she moved, he pulled her tighter against him. Finally, nature called and took precedence. She rolled out of his arms and went into the bathroom, then came back out, glancing at the clock. Five in the morning.

Griffin watched her through half-opened eyes. "Come back to bed."

"I need to get moving if I'm going to get the boys ready for school on time."

Griffin grabbed the back of her nightgown and reeled her back toward the bed. "I'm here to help. We'll do it in half the time together."

"I appreciate your willingness to assist, but you have to get to work, too."

He turned her so she faced him and began working open the buttons on her nightgown while he kissed the dimple on her cheek. "For your information, I happen to enjoy helping you with the boys." He opened another button, dropped a kiss on her collarbone. "I actually enjoy helping *you*."

He opened another button and revealed the creamy skin just above her breast. He placed his lips there, and she couldn't hold back a moan.

"And mostly I want to help you so we can have time to do this before the day begins. So, what do you say?" He gazed up at her, his eyes warming to liquefied silver.

He slid the nightgown over her head and tossed it onto the floor, then pressed a kiss to her belly.

"I say you were forewarned, so if you don't like the crazy rush of getting the kids ready, too bad," she told him.

Griffin kissed the inside of her thigh, and she shuddered in response.

The man certainly knew how to get a morning off to a bang.

15

A week after the snowstorm, most of the snow had melted away. The roads were clear, and warmer weather was forecast for the next week.

Cassie picked up the boys from school and headed back to Sittin' Pretty. "The social worker is coming tomorrow, and all you have to do is talk to her. Nothing else. Okay?"

"Why do we have to talk to another social worker?" Tyler demanded.

Cassie didn't miss the anger and fear behind the question, but she remained calm and unruffled. "In order for me to keep you guys, we have to go through this to show that I will provide a good home. This is your chance to tell the social worker how you feel about staying with me."

She pulled into the Beauty Bowl and parked the car then faced all three boys buckled in the backseat. "If this isn't what you want, it's your chance to say so. You have a voice in this." She looked at each child. "I want us to be a family."

"What about Dad?" Jeff asked.

"He'll always be your dad, but he can't make decisions for you. I hope he will choose to be part of your life."

Tyler's dark eyes grew fierce. "He's never coming back. He doesn't want us. We were always in his way."

She calmly looked at Tyler, hearing his anger. Deep down she knew fear lurked. She'd experienced that fear and understood it. "Right now he can't come for you, but I hope someday he'll be able to be your dad again. I know this is scary, but all you have to do is tell the social worker the truth. Where you want to live and who you want to live with."

Tyler stared out the window, resentment oozing from him. "Okay."

Trevor and Jeff nodded in agreement.

Tyler shoved open the car door. "I'm going to play video games." He hopped out of the car before Cassie could say anything else.

"Me, too," Jeff said and followed his brother.

Trevor was silent a long moment as he stared at Cassie. "You can tell them whatever you want, but I know Dad's not coming back. Jeff doesn't remember much, but me and Tyler do. Dad was harder on us, especially Tyler. He's scared the social worker will send us back to Dad. That's why he's angry all the time."

What had her cousin said to his sons? Cassie would find a way to help them overcome whatever damage Raymond had done.

Trevor started to climb out of the car then stopped. "Just so you know, I don't want to be anywhere but here with you."

Cassie blinked back tears as Trevor got out of the car and went inside. She would do everything within her power to give them the home they deserved.

CAROLYN MCNEIL, the social worker, arrived the next morning. The woman was professional, warm with the kids, and kind from Cassie's observations.

Ms. McNeil did an appraisal of the house, obviously looking to see how clean it was or wasn't, and then she spoke with each boy privately.

Even with Cassie's reassurances about the investigation, the boys were still upset, and justifiably so. Their lives had been turned upside down when Raymond left them, and she had no way of preventing that from happening again.

After she finished interviewing the kids, the woman spoke to Cassie.

"Ms. Cooper, I can tell that you've worked very hard to provide a good home for these children. That's commendable, particularly since I'm assuming that there was a bit of a learning curve as a single parent."

Nerves had Cassie's stomach tied in knots. She exhaled and forced a smile. "That's a major understatement, but we've all learned as we've gone along. And while it's been a huge adjustment, I can't imagine my life without them." Every word was the truth. She loved them as fiercely as their mother, Maria, had.

The social worker reviewed her notes. "The boys mentioned that you're dating a man named Griffin Valentine."

"That's correct."

"I'll need to speak with him."

"That won't be a problem." She gave her Griffin's contact information.

"Is your relationship serious?"

Her question gave Cassie a moment's pause. It was for her and she hoped Griffin felt the same. "We're a couple, if that's what you're asking."

She nodded. "It is. Does he stay here—overnight?"

"Yes. Is that a problem?"

"Not unless there's some reason he'd be considered a bad influence."

A genuine smile crossed Cassie's face. "No."

The social worker scribbled down some more notes, then rose. "That's all I have for now."

Cassie showed her out then sagged back against the door and prayed she would be approved.

Tyler materialized at her side, his expression pinched and his body tense. "We'll be good. We won't fight, I promise. Just don't let them take us away."

Cassie tilted his chin so she could look him in the eye. "I'm not letting anyone take you guys from me. And for the record, not that I wouldn't love for you to get along with your brothers, but I just want you to be you, nothing more. Do you understand?"

Tyler nodded and smiled. "Got it."

Cassie pulled him into her arms and held him tight. She would move heaven and earth to keep them.

GRIFFIN HAD JUST FINISHED with a patient when his nurse, Dolores stuck her head in the door. "A social worker is here to speak with you."

"Send her back."

Griffin rose and came around his desk to meet the investigator at the door. They shook hands.

"I'm Carolyn McNeil." She handed him her card.

Griffin gestured to the chair in front of his desk. "Have a seat. Can I get you a cup of coffee or tea?" he asked.

"No, thank you."

Griffin sat down at his desk chair. As he waited for the first question, he'd never been so nervous in his life. What he said here today could make the difference between Cassie keeping the boys and losing them.

"Thank you for making time for me, Dr. Valentine. I know you have a busy schedule."

"I'm happy to answer any questions you have."

"Thank you. I understand you're dating Ms. Cooper. Is that correct?"

"Yes."

"What are your feelings toward the children?"

"I love them. They're great kids."

"Do you have children, Dr. Valentine?"

The question threw him. He could say no, and it would be the truth in that Bobby was gone, but it would feel like he was denying his son existed, and he couldn't do that. "I had a son. He died in a car accident two years ago."

The social worker glanced up at him, sympathy flickering in her eyes. "I'm very sorry for your loss."

Griffin stared at the framed picture of his son on the file cabinet, grinning back at him. The familiar sense of loss filled him, then it was gone.

"Ms. Cooper says that you two are in an exclusive relationship. Is that how you define it?"

The question forced him to rein in his sorrow. "Yes, definitely."

"How serious are you?"

What were his feelings for Cassie? She was the first person he thought of when he woke in the morning and the last before he fell asleep at night.

"We grew up together, but we've only been dating a few months, but I care very deeply for her."

"If she had full custody of the children, would that change your feelings about her?"

"Absolutely not. I consider them a package deal." And sometimes he wondered if the kids made her more attractive to him. The thought gave him pause.

The social worker made several notes, then picked up her bag and rose. "I think that's all I have for now, Dr. Valentine. I may have further questions."

"I'm available anytime," Griffin said. He escorted her out of the building then went back to his office and called Cassie, but the call went to voicemail. Rather than leave a message, he hung up. He'd talk to her this evening and fill her in on the interview. He just hoped the investigator had been satisfied with his comments because there was way too much riding on this for him to screw up.

16

Cassie had dinner well underway when Griffin and the boys got home that evening. He'd offered to pick Trevor up from basketball practice, and Tyler and Jeff from karate lessons.

Jeff charged inside. "Cassie look what I got." He held up a blue ribbon.

Cassie squatted down in front of him. "What's this for?"

"I won our spelling bee today."

She hugged him. "That's wonderful."

Tyler snorted. "Big deal."

Trevor nudged him, and Tyler nudged him back. A battle brewed, but Griffin stepped between them. He gave them each a long look, and both boys immediately subsided.

How did he do that? She needed to acquire that ability. No, what she needed was to stop deferring to Griffin.

"I hope everybody's hungry. It's Mexican tonight."

"Why don't you boys go wash up, and then you can help set the table." Griffin said. They started off for the bathroom. "And take your things with you," he called after them.

The instant they were gone, he took Cassie in his arms and gave her a welcome home kiss. "How was your day?" he asked.

She melted against him, contentment filling her. She liked being held after a long day. They fit.

"Better now that I've had a kiss from you."

"If that's all it takes to improve your day, I'll make this an everyday occurrence," Griffin promised.

Cassie pressed tighter against him. "I may just take you up on that." Was that sexy rasp coming from her?

The timer dinged. Cassie slipped out of his arms and went over to the stove to check on dinner.

"I spoke with the investigator today."

Cassie froze and slowly faced him. "How did it go?"

Griffin took plates from the cupboard and began setting the table. "From what I could tell, fine."

The boys came back, ending their discussion. She didn't want to worry them any more than they already were. Cassie placed dinner on the table.

Griffin and the boys cleaned up after they finished eating, since she'd cooked. There was plenty of groaning, but Griffin ignored it.

"The person who does the cooking doesn't do cleanup."

"Then I want to cook tomorrow night," Jeff piped up.

"That could be arranged," Griffin said. "What do you plan on making for us?"

Jeff pondered his question, then brightened, a smile engulfing his face. "Hot dogs."

"We can have hot dogs," Griffin said. "But not every time you cook. Sometimes you're going to have to make things that take longer to prepare."

"I only know how to make hot dogs."

"Why don't you think about something you'd like to learn how to make, and I'll teach you?"

What couldn't this man do, Cassie wondered.

He's a keeper.

No question about that, but did he want to be?

CASSIE GOT HOME SHORTLY before noon and was about to make lunch when the doorbell rang. Chet stood on the porch with Rookie at his side.

Rookie nudged her hand, staring at her with those eyes that reached deep into her soul.

She smiled and held the door wide, gesturing for them to come inside. She took Chet's coat.

He stared at her, saying nothing for a long moment, his blue eyes sweeping over her—the exact blue as hers.

"I brought lunch." He held up a paper bag.

The smells wafting from the bag had her mouth watering, especially when the lunch she'd planned was cheese and saltine crackers.

She led him to the kitchen. "Coffee?" she asked.

"Yes, thanks."

"Have a seat." She filled two mugs and set them on the table.

Rookie laid down at her feet as Chet began unloading the bag. Cassie's stomach made an appreciative rumble when she recognized food from Little Italy.

"I hope you like meatball sandwiches."

Her favorite. Someone must have been feeding him information. Chet Cooper had a magnetism about him that was impossible to resist, and she wasn't immune to it as much as she'd liked to think.

Cassie added sugar and plenty of cream to her coffee. "I assume someone at Little Italy told you this is my favorite sandwich?"

Chet's expression turned sheepish. "I might have made an inquiry or two."

Good to know he wasn't a mind reader.

Cassie unwrapped her sandwich, took a bite, and the flavors burst in her mouth. She sighed. "Delicious."

"You're probably wondering what I'm doing here."

Cassie nodded.

"Since I'm going to be living here for the indefinite future, I was hoping we could get to know each other. You have a good life and a family. You don't have any reason to know me. Frankly, my reasons are selfish. I have no one—other than you. But I understand you're hesitant."

Cassie wiped her fingers on a paper napkin, watching as he bit into his sandwich.

Did she really want to turn away the man she'd spent a lifetime worshipping from afar?

Rookie laid his chin on her thigh and stared at her.

Why was she hesitating?

Fear—whether it was gaining custody of the boys or getting to know her father. No more. She wouldn't allow it to rule her life any longer.

Cassie decided honesty was the best way to proceed. "What do you say we start by having lunch together on Mondays?"

The blue in his eyes deepened—the same exact way she'd seen it so many times when he'd made a spectacular play or hit a home run.

"I'd like that very much."

Cassie watched him closely and sensed sincerity.

"Tell me about your job with the Cornhuskers."

Chet told her about his plans for the team, the players he'd been scouting, and the prospects he was hoping to sign. Obviously, he loved coaching and was anxious for the season to begin, even though it was still five months away. He was as addicted to baseball as Sam and Griffin. Not that she didn't enjoy a good baseball game, but she didn't have the same obsession with the sport that most of her family did. For her, it was just a way to while away a summer afternoon.

They discussed everything but their relationship, which was probably for the best. Getting to know each before dipping into the powder keg of emotions was a good starting point. They could see where they went after that.

~

CASSIE FINISHED READING JEFF A STORY.

"Cassie, are we gonna have to leave you?"

How did she answer him without lying or frightening him with her own uncertainty?

"I know what's happening is scary, but I'm doing this so that you can stay here with me forever." She hugged Jeff tight. "I love you guys so much."

Jeff's small arms squeezed her neck. "I love you, too. I don't ever wanna leave." He pulled back, his dark eyes round with concern. "Tyler says they might make us leave."

Cassie cupped his small cheeks between her hands and looked deeply into his eyes. "No one is making you leave. Got that?"

Jeff grinned, snuggled into his pillow, and closed his eyes. A few reassuring words and he was content, but not the same for Trevor and Tyler. They were old enough to remember being bounced from one dilapidated apartment to another. She would have to have a heart-to-heart with them tomorrow.

Cassie turned off the light and went to her bedroom. The shower was running, and Griffin belted out a rock song from the eighties about sex and wild women. The man had a set of vocal chords that radiated raw sex.

The water shut off as Cassie changed into her nightgown and crawled into bed. She checked her phone and saw an email from her attorney.

Griffin stepped out of the bathroom with just a towel wrapped around his waist. Cassie gave him an admiring once-over.

"Do I meet with your approval?" He leaned against the doorjamb and flexed his right arm, drawing a laugh from her.

"Oh, definitely."

She laid her phone on the nightstand and crossed over to him.

"Something important on your phone?"

"A message from Mark."

"And?" Griffin asked.

"He doesn't anticipate any problems with me gaining custody. He's trying to contact Raymond. So far, no luck."

"That sounds promising."

Cassie shrugged. "Maybe, but I still worry."

"Everything's going to work out."

Cassie's gaze shot up. "You can't know that. Raymond could come back for the kids. He's their father, and the courts will give them back to him."

"Doubtful. He abandoned them, and he has addiction problems."

All true, but he was still their father and that would give him a lot of sway with the court.

Griffin tugged her into his arms. "Stop worrying, everything will work out."

Cassie rested her hands on his chest. "Thank you."

"For what?"

"For being my sounding board and my support."

His eyes twinkled. "It's my pleasure."

She threaded her fingers into his hair, then pressed her lips to his.

Drawing her close, he deepened the kiss.

Her pulse quickened, and conscious thought evaporated as passion ignited a fire inside her that only Griffin could extinguish.

CONTENTMENT FILLED Griffin as he held Cassie, her head tucked into the crook of his neck. Having someone to hold—just the presence of another human being next to him at night—filled the emptiness in his soul.

"I heard you and Chet had lunch today."

She tensed. "How did you hear that?"

"We had a meeting at Cornhusker field, and Chet mentioned it in passing."

"Oh." When she didn't elaborate, Griffin trailed his fingers down her arm. "I know you're being cautious with him, but I hope spending time with him works out for you."

She twisted to look up at him. "Me, too. I just wish I was certain of his motivations."

"I wish I could answer that, but you'll have to decide on your own. Trust your instincts. You'll know."

She was silent for a long moment. "I'm just not sure I need this in my life right now. Not with trying to get custody of the boys."

Griffin considered her comment. "Maybe he's exactly what you need. He supports you, and you can't have too much support, can you? One thing I know for certain is you won't know unless you give him a shot."

"I hate it when you make sense," she grumbled.

Griffin tapped the end of her nose, chuckling.

Cassie nudged him. "Smugness does not become you."

Before he could respond, the bedroom door flew open and small feel scrambled across the carpet before Jeff launched himself between them, wrapping his arms around Griffin's neck.

Griffin rubbed his back. "What's wrong, buddy?"

"I had a bad dream."

Cassie murmured soothing words to him as she brushed the hair from his forehead. "Can you tell us about it?" she asked.

Jeff shook his head and buried his face in Griffin's chest.

"Talking about it can help sometimes," Griffin said.

"No!"

They waited for him to calm down, and when he finally did, he reached for Cassie. She hugged him close. "It's okay. I won't let anything hurt you."

"I don't wanna leave you, Cassie."

Jeff's body shuddered, and Cassie continued to hold him close. "Everything's going to be okay. You don't need to worry. I'm going to make sure you're taken care of."

Griffin leaned down so that his face was next to Jeff's. "Cassie and I have your back. She's never let you down, has she?"

Jeff raised his head, his eyes still dark with fear. Finally, he shook his head.

"You can count on her."

Cassie looked over Jeff's head at Griffin, her eyes so soft and warm he wanted to curl into them.

"It's going to be okay, Jeff," she said again. He snuggled into her, and within minutes his breathing evened out as sleep overtook him.

The moment reminded Griffin of the times he'd held Bobby when he'd been upset—and he cherished those memories. When they were certain Jeff was asleep, Griffin carried him back to his bed. He straightened to find Trevor and Tyler standing in the doorway, wide-eyed and clearly upset.

Cassie came alongside them and put an arm around each boy. She turned them toward their bedroom. "Everything's going to be okay."

Griffin would do everything in his power to help her keep that promise.

17

C assie got the kids to school the next morning, then stopped at Death Wish, Betsy McGuire's drive-through coffee stand. Betsy made coffee at an octane level that could keep you going all day long, and Cassie desperately needed a shot today if she was going to keep up with her full load of clients. She paid for two cups of coffee then headed to work.

She entered the Beauty Bowl and saw Bettina "Dragon Lady" Hardgrave waiting impatiently outside Sittin' Pretty—a full thirty minutes early. She would expect Cassie to take her in early, too.

Wasn't going to happen. Bettina had a weave, cut, and style scheduled at nine. That's when Cassie would start and not a second before.

Cassie made a detour for the kitchen, smiling and nodding at several regulars sitting at the bar. She pushed open the double stainless steel doors and found her aunt behind the grill.

Cassie set one cup of coffee next to her aunt and placed hers on the center table, then grabbed an apron. "Where's Donnie?"

"I sent him home. He was burning up with fever and coughing up enough phlegm to drive away even my most loyal customers." Her aunt picked up the coffee, took a sip, and sighed. "God bless you. I needed a cup of Betsy's finest today."

Cassie tapped her cup to her aunt's. "I wish I could fill in for the whole day, but I've got a full schedule."

"Don't you worry about me. Laverne's on her way."

Cassie resisted the urge to roll her eyes. Laverne was as sweet as the day was long, but the poor woman was irreparably scatterbrained.

"At least I can fill in for the next thirty minutes since my first appointment isn't until nine."

"I thought I saw Bettina come through ten minutes ago."

Cassie grinned. "You did, but I don't open until nine, and I intend to enjoy my coffee and wait on customers until then."

Aunt Luella laughed and tapped her cup to Cassie's again. "Salute."

Cassie took another gulp of her coffee then grabbed a pad and pen and went out to take orders. For the next twenty minutes she delivered food, filled coffee cups, and bussed tables. Just when it was time to open the shop, Laverne arrived and replaced her.

Cassie heard a few groans as she handed her apron over to the older woman. Fortunately Laverne was not only scatterbrained, but hard of hearing as well.

Cassie refilled her coffee then grabbed her purse. Before she could escape, Walt Burgan touched her arm.

"You aren't really going to leave us here with Laverne, are you?"

She patted Walt's hand. He'd been a friend of her Uncle Albert's and never had a bad word to say about anyone. "Sorry, I've got a customer waiting at the salon."

Walt grunted. "Let Bettina wait. Might teach her some patience."

Cassie laughed. "I doubt it."

"Me, too."

"If I get served before noon, can you squeeze me in for a haircut?"

Cassie pressed a kiss to his cheek then whispered in his ear, "Always." She slipped away and went to face the dragon lady.

"You're late," Bettina snipped as Cassie unlocked the door.

Cassie glanced at the clock that read eight fifty-eight. "Actually, I'm two minutes early. Have a seat and I'll be right with you."

Bettina harrumphed, hung up her coat and purse, then stomped over to the vacant styling chair. "Your clock is slow."

"Really, by how much?" Cassie called from the back room where she put away her purse and grabbed an apron.

"Two minutes."

Bettina was obnoxiously prompt and felt everyone should arrive thirty minutes in advance.

"Well, I'll have to reset the clock." Cassie forced a smile even though she'd prefer to send Bettina on her way. "So, what are we doing today?"

"The usual."

Bettina had worn the same pageboy style for decades. In all fairness, it was a good, classic look for her, but Cassie would go nuts if she didn't change her hairstyle every now and again.

As she mixed the color for Bettina's hair, she endured every petty complaint from Bettina's three-minute wait at the grocery store to the newspaper carrier who was ten minutes late on Monday because he had a flat tire—which was no excuse for tardiness in Bettina's opinion. He should have checked the tires the night before.

By the time Cassie finished coloring, cutting, drying, and styling Bettina's hair, she was more than ready for the next customer. Not that Bettina noticed, but Cassie had finished in record time and had fifteen minutes to spare before her next appointment. And as luck would have it, Walt strolled in.

"Perfect timing. Take a seat while I clean up."

Walt settled his angular frame into the chair.

"So, did you get breakfast?"

His scowl reflected in the mirror. "In a manner of speaking."

Cassie dumped the hair she'd swept up into the garbage can, then met Walt's mildly annoyed gaze.

"I got an order of pancakes that belonged to Mildred Hatfield. Then a Denver omelet that was supposed to be Rancheros Huevos. By the time I got my eggs and bacon, they were cold and missing the whole wheat toast—plus I ended up refilling my own coffee and about five others."

"I'm sorry. You know Aunt Luella would have made you more."

Walt's eyes twinkled. "I do and I will get payback when it's not so crazy," he teased.

Why did Cassie suspect that Walt was referring to more than food? Not a question she wanted to ask or have answered.

"I shared a cup of coffee with the new head coach of the Cornhuskers. Seems like a good fella." The curiosity burning in Walt's eyes told her they'd talked about more than coaching.

Why did everyone feel compelled to comment on her personal life?

"So I've heard."

"It's nice to have some new blood in town."

She grunted and didn't disagree with him as she ran a comb through his silver mane.

"Could have blown me over with a feather when he told me he was your dad."

Cassie froze, her eyes meeting Walt's. "He said what?"

Walt grinned, completely unaware of her negative reaction. "That he's your dad."

"How exactly did that come up?"

Walt pondered her question. "Well, we were drinking coffee and discussing baseball, and I asked him how he ended up in Hope's Crossing of all places. He told me he came to see his daughter, and I said who's your daughter, and he said Cassie Cooper."

There was never a short answer with Walt, which gave Cassie time to pull herself together.

"So, is he your dad?"

"Yes, he is."

He winked at her. "Well, I'm just pleased as punch to hear that. A girl's never too old to need her dad."

Or her mother, Cassie silently added. Maybe getting to know Chet would be a good thing after all.

She'd just finished cutting Walt's hair when her next appointment arrived. The rest of the morning passed in a blur, but she couldn't forget Walt's words about a girl needing her dad. The more she got to know Chet, the more she wanted him in her life.

GRIFFIN'S MORNING started with Molly Burkhart and her six-year-old son, Timmy, who sprained his wrist when he fell off his bicycle. That was followed by three cases of the most recent virus making the rounds. His best advice—stay home, rest, and drink plenty of fluids.

With a short break between patients, he went back to his office for a cup of coffee and to relax for a few minutes. He leaned back in his chair and stared at the photo of Bobby on the file cabinet. An ache settled deep in Griffin's chest. The anniversary of Bobby's death was coming up in a few weeks.

Dolores came barreling into his office, and the past vanished.

"We have an emergency, Doc."

Griffin shoved out of his chair, pushing his emotions aside and focusing on the patient. "What happened?"

"Farming accident. Jim Hansen mangled his arm in the swather."

"Why didn't he call nine-one-one?"

"I told him to. He wouldn't listen. Insisted it wasn't that bad, and he wasn't about to drive to the hospital when he could come here."

Griffin swore under his breath. "These guys are so damn stubborn."

Dolores changed the paper on the table. "They are."

"How long do we have?"

"Jim just drove in," his receptionist yelled from her desk.

Griffin and Dolores raced to the front door just as Jim walked through, his arm wrapped in a towel, leaving a trail of blood up the walkway.

"Get him back to the exam room so I can see how bad this is."

Dolores ushered him back and got him on the table as Griffin unwrapped the towel.

"Call for an ambulance. This is going to need surgery."

The blood loss left Jim too weak to make more than a feeble objection.

Dolores helped Griffin pack the wound, and they had the bleeding under control when the paramedics arrived minutes later. They loaded Jim onto a stretcher and took him to the hospital.

~

CASSIE TOSSED and turned trying to sleep, but couldn't. She was worried about Griffin. He'd been so calm when he'd called to tell her he was on the way to the hospital to check on a patient. He hadn't told her who it was, but it was all over town that Jim Hansen had nearly lost his arm in the swather. She wished Griffin were here so she could offer him comfort and listen to his day as he'd done so frequently for her, but so far he'd hadn't given her a chance to return the favor.

Didn't being in a relationship mean supporting one another? It couldn't be a one-way street. Good relationships didn't work that way.

Griffin spent most nights here, and she'd come to depend on having him beside her to cuddle up to. With each passing day, she became more and more attached, but did Griffin feel the same way? It wasn't just herself she had to consider. She had three boys who thought of Griffin as their own personal superhero. If she and Griffin didn't make it, the boys would be crushed.

Cassie rolled onto her other side, felt the empty space on the bed, and wished Griffin were here beside her.

Grrrr.

She punched the pillow and tried to settle in, but her thoughts moved back to Griffin like a damned heat-seeking missile.

She looked at her phone. No calls or texts. She set it back on the nightstand and went to sleep.

~

IT WAS after midnight when Griffin walked into the doctor's lounge. The surgery had gone well, and the surgeon had been able to save Jim's arm.

The adrenaline had finally run out and Griffin was exhausted. He grabbed a cup of coffee, hoping the caffeine kept him alert for the drive home. He rubbed his eyes as headed out to his car. The emergency had kept his mind off the upcoming anniversary of Bobby's death, but the silent drive home brought the memories rushing in from all sides. All the events he'd missed or arrived late because of a surgery that had taken precedence over his family—the same as it had been when he was growing up. His father had always had a patient that had taken precedence over his wife and children.

The last time Griffin had put work before family had also been the last day he'd seen his son. He'd begged off going to the dinosaur exhibition with them. He'd just finished the knee surgery when a nurse came in to tell him his wife and son had been in an accident. As he'd raced to the elevator and took it down to the ER, he'd carefully pushed his emotions aside to deal with the crisis at hand. He pushed through the double glass doors, but he'd arrived too late.

Bobby was gone.

While Griffin couldn't have saved him, there was no doubt in his mind he should have been in the car with them. If he had, he would have been there to hold his son and say goodbye. Instead, he'd done elective surgery on a stranger.

What kind of parent did that make him?

In Mary's long list of grievances, he'd always neglected them, putting work first. He had followed his father's motto to the letter—career before family. And doing so, he'd failed Mary and Bobby, so what was he doing with Cassie and her boys? She deserved better than what he could offer her. He should walk away before history repeated itself and he let them down, too.

But that didn't stop him from going to the one place that offered him sanctuary from the demons that haunted him—Cassie's.

18

G riffin dropped his clothes on the floor and slid into bed, wrapping his arms around Cassie. All the way there he'd told himself to just go home, but he'd gone straight to Cassie instead. The truth that he didn't want to admit was, he needed her. Just that simple.

It was time he acknowledged the truth he'd been avoiding. He loved Cassie, and his feelings went deeper than anything he'd ever felt for Mary. He also loved the bickering and roughhousing—the commotion and constant racket that accompanied a houseful of boys—a stark comparison to his silent, empty house.

Cassie's supple body molded against him. And he held onto her as if she were his last breath.

Her voice groggy with sleep, she said, "Griffin?"

"It's me."

She shifted so she faced him, her breasts nestled against his chest. "I assumed you were going to your house."

"I was, then I decided I didn't want to be alone."

"Did something go wrong with the surgery?"

"It was long, but everything went fine."

Cassie blew out a sigh of relief. "That's good to hear." She pressed her cheek to his chest and snuggled closer. "I'm glad you're here. I missed you."

"I missed you too." Griffin kissed the top of her head, and the tension ebbed away. He drifted off to sleep, more content than he'd been in a long, long time.

～

CASSIE AWOKE a little after five the next morning, still nestled in Griffin's arms, his body warm and clearly aroused.

Her gaze traveled up to his face to find a pair of silver eyes dark with desire. "Have you got something in mind?" she asked.

"I just might."

"Well, I hope you're up for a quickie because the boys will be getting up soon."

"A quickie would fit the bill." He pulled her onto his chest and kissed her until thoughts of getting out of bed vanished. The boys could be late for school just this once.

～

CASSIE MANAGED to get the kids to school on time with a smile plastered on her face despite their incessant bickering. She even had a skip to her step, but it faded rapidly when she finished her first appointment and two walk-ins came in that put her behind schedule. She'd just finished the last one when the school called for her to pick up Jeff, who had a fever of a hundred and two. She had just enough time to get him before her next appointment arrived. She grabbed her purse and was about to walk out the door when Chet and Rookie entered.

She greeted him more abruptly than she intended. "I've got to go."

He took her hand before she could rush off. "What's wrong?"

"Jeff's sick. I've got to pick him up and get back before my ten o'clock appointment arrives."

"I was hoping we could have lunch today, but that's clearly out. Maybe I could pick up Jeff and stay with him until you can get away?"

Cassie's jaw went slack. "Have you taken care of a sick child before?"

"No, but I think I can manage for a couple of hours. If I have a problem I'll call."

Cassie hated to shut down the shop, but she couldn't leave Jeff at school either. "Okay. I'll be free by noon." She handed him her house keys, then took out her phone. "I'll call the school to let them know you'll be picking him up."

"I won't let you down."

She was putting her trust in him.

He started out the door, and Cassie called after him. "Thanks."

He waved and walked on before she could change her mind. She focused on clearing her schedule so she could get home to Jeff. Melissa Whitman, her next appointment arrived. She motioned for her to take a seat while she called the school.

CASSIE MANAGED to clear her afternoon and made it home a few minutes after twelve. She found Jeff on the sofa slurping chicken soup and watching a movie with Rookie nestled against his side. The medicine she'd told Chet to give him must have helped.

She pressed a kiss to his forehead. "How are you feeling?"

He shrugged. "My throat hurts, but the soup Chet made helps."

Rookie lifted his head, and she petted him.

"Where is Chet?"

Jeff pointed to the kitchen with his spoon, not looking away from the television.

"I'll be back."

Cassie walked in the kitchen and froze. Chet had not only made chicken soup, but he'd fixed grilled cheese sandwiches that smelled divine.

He turned and smiled at her. "Jeff was hungry so I made lunch. I hope you don't mind."

Mind? She was eternally grateful.

"Are you hungry?" he asked.

"Starving."

"Sit down."

Cassie pulled out a chair, and minutes later they were both eating. "This is delicious. I didn't know you could cook."

"I can, I just don't enjoy cooking for myself."

In other words, *alone*.

She squeezed his hand. "Thank you for helping me today."

Chet smiled, a warm, genuine smile. "I like helping with the boys." He set his sandwich down. "There's something else I'd like to discuss. I know it's none of my business, but Luella told me you're trying to get custody of the boys."

Her aunt couldn't keep a secret if it killed her.

Chet took her silence as permission to continue.

"What if your cousin decides he doesn't want to relinquish custody of them? Wouldn't it be prudent to gather any information you can on him?"

"Raymond wouldn't do that."

Those eyes she'd watched on television for decades pinned her. "You're talking about taking custody of his children. You don't know how he'll react."

Cassie wanted to believe Raymond wouldn't fight her for custody, but she couldn't, especially after her last conversation with him. The undeniable fact was, she was taking her cousin's children from him. Even though she knew it was best for the kids, she hated doing it, and she wasn't at all sure what Raymond would do.

Chet cleared his throat and she met his gaze. "I have money, enough to hire someone to look into him. Let me do this for you."

The offer took her by surprise. "Oh no, I can't. It's too much."

"Yes, you can. I want to help. Please let me do this."

Pride warred with common sense. How could she turn down a sincere offer of help? She couldn't—not when it came to the boys. Pushing aside her pride, she nodded.

"*Caaasssie.*"

She slid her chair back, hesitated a moment, then threw caution to the wind and hugged him. "Thank you," she said, then pressed a kiss his cheek.

There was still a part of her that feared he'd go back to his life and forget about her, but if that happened wasn't it better to have a little heartbreak than lose the opportunity of getting to know her father?

∽

GRIFFIN FINISHED work early and headed to Cassie's. She'd texted that Jeff was sick and she'd shut down the shop at noon.

He pulled into Cassie's driveway as Chet and Rookie were leaving. He waved, went inside, and found Cassie in the kitchen making a cup of tea.

He walked over to the sink and took her into his arms, hugging her close. He inhaled her fresh, clean scent. "I've missed you."

"You saw me this morning."

"But it feels like forever."

Cassie squeezed him. Finally, she pulled away, and they sat down at the table.

Griffin studied her as she sipped her tea. "I saw Chet leaving."

She nodded as she added a spoonful of sugar. "He picked up Jeff and took care of him until I could close the shop." She gestured to the pot on the stove. "He made chicken soup. There's plenty if you're hungry."

He was starving. He filled a bowl, and once he'd settled back beside her, she said, "Chet offered to hire a private investigator to do a background check on Raymond."

"Why?"

"Raymond already told me he'd fight me on custody, so finding him, getting background information on him, makes sense to me."

Griffin nodded. "That does make sense. So you've agreed to let Chet help you?"

"I did. I'm hoping if the PI finds Raymond, I can talk to him and explain what I'm doing and why. I hate that I have to do this. I want him to see the kids. He's their father."

"But?" Griffin asked.

Her brows furrowed. "But it scares me that I've made myself vulnerable with Chet by accepting his help," she said.

"It's a risk for sure, but it might be one worth taking for the boys' sakes." Griffin laid his cheek against her hair. "Everything will work out."

Cassie looked up at him, her eyes troubled. "Thanks, I really appreciate your support."

"You can always count on me."

"Can I?"

A cough, then, "*Caaasssi*e, I'm thirsty."

"Coming."

She rose, but Griffin eased her down into her chair. "What did you mean just now?"

Her gaze darted to the living room then back to him. "I'm not sure where we're going, but it feels like you shoulder everything. Don't get me wrong, I appreciate everything you do, but a good relationship should have give and take. I just seem to be doing all the taking and it makes me feel like you don't need me."

"*Caaasssi*e." Jeff's wail ended the conversation, much to Griffin's relief. But it was a temporary reprieve. At some point, he would have to open up to her or lose her.

19

A week later, Cassie and Griffin arrived at the rundown hotel outside of Indianapolis where the PI had found Raymond. They went to the room number she'd been given and knocked on the door. The television blared from inside, but no one answered.

Cassie knocked again, harder this time. "Raymond."

Silence, then finally some movement from inside. "Who is it?"

"Cassie."

"Go away."

She knocked on the door again, and Griffin stepped closer. "I need to talk to you about the boys."

A muttered oath, then more footsteps. Finally, the door opened a crack, and Raymond stared through the opening, first at Griffin then her. "Go home, Cassie. You shouldn't be here."

She held her ground. "Not until I talk to you."

He snorted. "You're taking my kids. I'm sure you won't have any problem getting custody."

She reached out and touched his arm. "I don't want it to be this way."

He glared at her. "Exactly how do you think it could be?"

She said nothing for a long moment. "Don't fight me on custody. They need stability, and this ensures they'll have a permanent home."

"With you and pretty boy here," Raymond sneered.

"No, me. I'm the one asking for custody."

"They're my kids."

Cassie exhaled heavily, trying to restrain her impatience. "I know. That's why I'm here. They love you and ask about you. I want them to know their father."

"But you'll have custody."

"Yes."

He stared at her a long minute, fury burning deep in his eyes, then it vanished and brown lifeless eyes stared back at her. "Go home, Cassie."

She reached out again and brushed his arm before he could close the door. He flinched, but she didn't back down. "Let me help you."

He barked out a caustic laugh. "Help me, how?"

"Rehab."

He shook his head. "You're the eternal optimist, aren't you?"

"If you're asking if I believe you can get clean, then yes I do."

Something akin to hope flickered in his eyes, then it was gone. "Fuck rehab."

He slammed the door in her face.

She'd hoped to reach him, but he didn't want help.

Griffin wrapped an arm around her shoulders and tucked her tight against him as he led her back to his truck. He helped her into the cab and didn't speak until they were away from the hotel.

"I'm sorry. I know you were hoping for a different outcome."

She stared out the window and watched the barren landscape. A tear slipped past her defenses, and she angrily brushed it aside. She'd shed enough tears over Raymond. She'd done all she could for him. Now she had to focus on what was best for the boys.

～

A WEEK LATER, Griffin escorted Cassie to his truck for the special evening he'd planned. She'd been down ever since they'd gone to see Raymond. A romantic evening with Griffin was just what she needed.

"You two have a good time and don't worry about a thing. I have everything under control," Luella called after them.

Cassie waved to her then climbed into the truck. All Griffin had told her was to dress warm. Other than that, she had no idea where they were going, which left her uneasy. A planner at heart, she wanted to know every detail, to be prepared for every contingency.

The fading afternoon sunlight washed the landscape in burnished fall colors of yellow, orange, and brown as Griffin pulled away from her house. Cows grazed on fields of corn stubble as they headed north toward Chicago.

"Where are we going?"

A dimple creased his left cheek. "Did you know there's a full Hunter's Moon tonight?" he asked instead of answering her question.

Cassie gazed out the window. What did the full moon have to do with where they were going? "No, I didn't know. Why is that important?"

"Well, a Hunter's Moon is special. It's also known as a sanguine or blood moon. The term Hunter's Moon is generally referred to as the full moon that appears in October, except once every four years when it doesn't appear until November. And this is that year.

"It got its name because during the month of October, hunters tracked and killed prey by autumn moonlight, stockpiling food for winter."

"Another unique aspect," Griffin continued before Cassie could interrupt, "is the moon rises fifty minutes later each day. But with the Hunter's Moon and the Harvest Moon that rise in September, they both rise thirty minutes later each successive night. What this means is that the sunset and moonrise are very close."

"You are just a wealth of information, but why do I suspect you're using that to divert me from asking about our date tonight?"

Griffin shrugged. "Just making conversation." The twinkle in his eye said otherwise. Wherever they were headed, she'd bet it had some connection to the full moon.

Thirty minutes later, Griffin turned west.

"Where are we going?" Cassie asked again.

He glanced at her, amusement dancing in his eyes. "You are relentless."

"I am, so you might as well tell me."

"Okay, we're eating at the Dunes."

Cassie faced him. "Really? Isn't the restaurant closed for the season?"

"It is."

"Then how are we going to eat there?"

"I never said we were."

Before she could grill him further, they arrived at the shores of Big Star Lake just as the sun dipped over the horizon turning the sky shades of fuchsia and deep, deep purple. Griffin parked and turned off the truck then faced her. "Wait here while I get things set up."

"Can I help?"

"No. When you plan a date, it's all yours. This one is mine. Now close your eyes, relax, and wait here until I come for you."

"This is silly," she muttered but closed her eyes. In truth, she loved it. She might be a planner, but she also loved surprises, particularly clever ones.

The tailgate dropped, and banging and thumping ensued. Several minutes later he came around to her door and told her to open her eyes. Griffin escorted her to the beach, where he'd built a bonfire. He'd also set up a table and two chairs with paper plates, two plastic wine glasses, and pizza. Not just any pizza—Giordano's.

She squealed, spinning a circle, then leaned over the box and inhaled through the closed lid. "Oh my God, the smell is amazing." She looked up at Griffin. "I love Giordano's pizza. How did you get it here?"

He pretended to zip his mouth closed. "I've been sworn to silence." He pulled out a chair for her, and she sat down. Wine?"

"I'd love some."

Soft music played from his phone as he poured her a glass. A gentle breeze ruffled Cassie's hair. She inhaled and savored the mix of wood smoke from the bonfire, damp sand, and clean, crisp air that emanated from Griffin. The man certainly knew how to create a romantic setting.

"We can eat dinner and watch the Hunter's Moon rise over the water."

Her stomach rumbled in a most unromantic way.

Griffin smiled. "I'm guessing you're ready to eat."

"I am."

He took the pizza from the insulated container and lifted the lid. Cassie's mouth watered as the scent of sausage, onions, and peppers filled the air. She forgot about everything except eating as he served her a slice of pizza that hung over both sides of the plate.

"My favorite. How did you know?"

Griffin put two slices on his plate and sat down. He winked. "I have my sources."

She shot him a mock frown. "Aren't you Mr. Mysterious tonight?"

The huge expanse of sky glowed in shades of lilac. Cassie took a bite of her pizza and savored the flavors and the view.

She studied him in the flickering firelight. She loved him and wanted to take that next step and tell him, but she hesitated. She'd promised herself she would take it slow and let their relationship evolve—after all they'd only been dating two months. But in that time, Griffin had shared almost nothing about himself.

"So, how's the pizza?"

"It's fantastic," she said and meant it.

They finished their meal, then Griffin added more wood to the fire. Shoulders brushing, they sat side-by-side on a sleeping bag sipping their wine. The moon rose, the orange glow shimmering across the water until it came right up to their fire.

Cassie sighed, soaking in the scene. The waves gently lapped against the shore; a flock of geese honked overhead, flying into the glowing orange moon. "This is so beautiful." She forgot about Raymond and the impending court battle. It was just her and Griffin.

"I hope you saved room for dessert—chocolate cake from Formento's."

"Even if I hadn't, I would still make room for that!" Formento's made the most obscenely wicked chocolate cake in all of Chicago.

He opened the box, and Cassie had to keep from drooling. "You keep feeding me like this, and I'll be doing double time at the gym."

Griffin's gaze slowly traveled over her body. "You'll always be perfect to me."

The compliment warmed her inside and out. He cut into the cake and offered her a bite. His fingers brushed her lower lip as she accepted the offering. The flavors burst in her mouth, a mixture of crushed hazelnuts, chocolate pudding frosting, and chocolate ganache. A perfect blend of confections.

She sighed. "This is to die for."

Griffin took a bite. The action of this throat working hypnotized her, and she wanted to run her lips down the long column of his neck.

The fire crackled as he offered her another bite, and she shivered as if he'd touched her intimately. Decadent bordering on indecent—the only way she could describe the scandalously rich dessert. Cassie took one more bite, savoring it, then rubbed her stomach. "That was amazing, but I can't eat any more."

Griffin ate a little more, then folded the lid closed. "We'll save it for tomorrow."

"If the boys see it, they'll devour it in seconds."

"Then we'll just have to put it somewhere they can't find it."

"Huh. Better encase it in lead to keep them from sniffing it out."

Griffin's deep laugher drifted on the night air. "Then I'll wrap it in a broccoli bag. They won't open that no matter how it smells." His eyes gleamed in the firelight. "Besides, I have plans for the rest of this cake that don't necessarily include eating it in the traditional way."

Goosebumps rose over her flesh that had nothing to do with the cold.

He rose, drew her into his arms, and danced cheek-to-cheek with her, his voice crooning in her ear as he sang along with the music.

"You are the one I've searched for all my life. You are perfect for me."

His arms tightened around her as he slowly swung her in a circle.

"I found the one woman for me. She's perfect for me. She's the one I can share everything with."

Cassie absorbed the lyrics, drawing them deep inside, wishing he spoke from the heart instead of just singing the words.

"I'm dancing in the dark with the woman of my dreams, and she's my angel."

The song ended, but he kept his arms around her, swaying as the moonlight shone over them and the bonfire burned hot and bright.

His hands wound into her hair. Gently lifting her head, he kissed her, his tongue sweeping inside her mouth. Despite the chill coming off the water, Cassie felt the burn of desire.

Griffin growled. "I want you more than I've ever wanted you before."

She groaned. "I'm yours."

He swept her into his arms and fulfilled her every wish.

CASSIE CURLED INTO GRIFFIN, snug and warm inside the sleeping bag. Her eyes grew drowsy, and her body relaxed. The logs shifted and sent sparks into the sky. Moonlight shimmered over the water—a perfect evening and one she wouldn't forget.'

Her phone dinged with a text, and the real world intruded. She wanted to ignore it, but she couldn't.

She grabbed her phone from her coat pocket. Trevor's name scrolled across the screen.

When are you coming home?

Not sure. Why?

My stomach hurts.

"What's wrong?" Griffin asked.

"Trevor's got an upset stomach."

"Do you have any soda?"

Cassie shook her head. "I don't keep it in the house, but there's sparkling water in the fridge."

"See if he'll drink that."

She texted Trevor and waited. No response. She dialed her aunt's phone.

Luella answered. "You're supposed to be on a date. Why are you calling?

"Trevor texted me he's not feeling well."

"Aunt Luella, I'm gonna be sick." Trevor's cry carried over the line followed by pounding footsteps, then the unmistakable sound of regurgitation.

Cassie's stomach rebelled, but she ignored it. "That sounds like more than a stomachache."

"Don't you worry about it. I've got everything under control."

"Aunt Luella, I'm gonna be sick," Tyler called out.

"Gotta go."

The line went dead.

Wonderful. The stomach flu.

She turned to find Griffin listening. "I'm sorry. I need to get home."

He drew her closer, so her breasts cradled against his chest. His breath warmed her face. "There's nothing to apologize for. There are sick children that need attention. They take precedence." He kissed the tip of her nose then released her. They dressed, and Griffin put out the fire while Cassie started loading the truck.

Within minutes they were headed back to the house.

Cassie touched his arm. "I just want you to know I had a wonderful time this evening."

Griffin raised her hand and kissed her palm. "I'm glad. We'll do it again."

Cassie studied him in the glow of the dash lights. Here was a man who offered her everything she'd ever wanted—romance and passion, and more than that, a man she could rely on, something he'd proven time and again. If only he would open up to her.

20

L uella met them at the door, looking frazzled. She huffed out a breath. "I told you it was nothing to worry about. You didn't need to come home."

"I'm not doubting your abilities. I just felt I needed to be here for the boys."

Her aunt relaxed. "Mothering instinct. I understand that."

"Aunt Luella." Trevor's voice came out more like a groan.

"With Griffin here, I guess you don't need me." She grabbed her purse, slipped on her coat, then hugged Cassie goodbye.

"Thank you for coming."

She waved off Cassie's gratitude. "I love taking care of them."

"Aunt Luella." Tyler's cry echoed down the hallway. "I'm gonna puke."

"Go on. I'll talk to you tomorrow."

Cassie closed the door, dropping her purse on the sofa before heading down the hallway.

Griffin marveled at how efficiently she handled the latest crisis. When the boys had first arrived she would've been overwhelmed— incapable of handling even the most simple situation, but now she took charge with ease.

In fact, she didn't need him. She could manage on her own just fine. So, why didn't he just leave? Selfishness—a primal need to be needed. It was what had drawn him to Mary. She couldn't function without him—or so he'd thought until she divorced him.

"Griffin," Cassie called, "could you run to the store for me?" She might be able to manage on her own, but that didn't mean she couldn't use some help.

He went to the bathroom where she knelt next to Tyler. "Sure, what do you need?"

"I'll make a list." To Tyler, she whispered, "I'll be right back." She pushed to her feet and went to the kitchen. After scribbling down the things she needed on a piece of paper, she gave Griffin a peck on the cheek before hurrying back to Tyler.

As Griffin drove off, he realized his relationship with Cassie was a whole lot more than just her needing him. She breathed life into him and the truth was, he'd be lost without her.

THE BOYS finally fell into a fitful sleep sometime after midnight. Fortunately, Jeff hadn't contracted the bug—yet—and hopefully he wouldn't. Two kids with the stomach flu was plenty. Cassie had enough soiled towels and sheets for three days worth of laundry.

Griffin had concocted something for them to drink that seemed to settle their stomachs. She'd have to find out what that was for future reference.

Collapsing on the sofa, her eyes drifted closed, then snapped open when the sour scent of bile filled the room. Wrinkling her nose, she shoved to her feet to start a load of laundry and hopefully rid the house of the odor before she became ill herself.

She pushed the start button on the washer. Nothing happened. She tried a second time. Still nothing.

"No." She kicked the machine. "You hunk of junk. How dare you fail me now?" This was the absolute last thing she needed.

Griffin came up behind her and massaged her shoulders. "Something wrong?"

"Yeah. This thing has decided to quit on me—when the house reeks of vomit."

"Go sit down. I'll look at it and see if I can get it going."

Cassie faced him, his silver eyes full of warmth and understanding. "You've done enough. I can't ask you to do this, too."

"You didn't ask, I offered."

Cassie brushed a lock of hair from his forehead. "Have I ever told you just how terrific you are?"

Griffin managed a smile. "You have, but I don't mind hearing it again."

"Well, you are, and I should tell you more frequently." She pressed a kiss to his lips. "But I have a better idea. Let's move the laundry out to the garage and deal with this tomorrow."

Griffin didn't object. "That sounds like a better plan."

Cassie scooped up the laundry basket full of sheets, dropping her voice to a husky rasp. "You do know there's nothing sexier than a handyman."

Griffin arched a brow. "Is that a fact?"

"It is. They always talk about how to marry a millionaire. I say it's the handyman you want."

"So, you're looking to marry a handyman?" His voice came out in a slow drawl that made her think of warm summer nights and scorching-hot sex.

"If I were—" She wiggled her hips and let the sentence hang.

"I'll keep that in mind." He leaned in for a kiss. Their lips barely touched when Tyler called from the bedroom.

Cassie sighed. "Looks like the reprieve is over."

"You go take care of Tyler. I'll get rid of this laundry and spray some air freshener to get rid of the smell, then I'll be in to help you."

Cassie wanted to insist he go home and get some rest, but the truth was, she wanted him here. Selfish for sure, but the truth was she loved him and wanted him by her side through sickness and health.

CASSIE SPENT the weekend knee-deep in vomit and sick children. Jeff eventually came down with it, too. It wasn't until Sunday before the kids were all feeling back to normal again, but by then Cassie's stomach was queasy, and not from the lingering scent of vomit permeating the house. She looked over at Griffin, who had collapsed on the sofa beside her. If she wasn't mistaken, his face had taken on a pasty color that didn't bode well for either of them.

"I don't know about you, but I think we've caught what the boys had."

Griffin swallowed and turned his head toward her. He pressed his fingers to her forehead. "You've got a fever."

Cassie laid the back of her hand to his cheek. "So do you."

"Ain't parenting grand?"

His attempt at humor drew a weak smile from her that turned into a grimace. Her stomach pitched as if she'd taken a quick descent on a rollercoaster. A second later, she raced for the bathroom.

CASSIE LAID on the bathroom floor and prayed for death. Finally, she found the strength to drag herself to the bed and laid down next to Griffin. She rolled her head to look at him. His face looked as gray and colorless as the overcast sky outside. And she'd thought taking care of the kids was the worst part. Ha!

Easy-peasy in comparison to actually heaving nonstop.

"How are you doing?" Griffin asked.

"About as good as you look."

He grimaced. "That bad, huh?"

"Oh yeah, I'm ready to go out dancing. How about you?"

"Name the time and place."

Cassie closed her eyes. "I'm up for anything just so long as I don't have to move off of this bed," she said, then drifted into oblivion.

THE NEXT MORNING Cassie managed to drag herself out of bed and get the kids ready for school. Griffin decided to go to work, but his face remained pale and his eyes were ringed with fatigue. He drove the boys to school so she could wait for the repairman. She'd paid extra to guarantee that he came this morning.

Cassie made a pot of broth while she waited for the repairman to arrive. It was almost noon before the washer was up and running. The instant he left, she started a load of laundry then collapsed on the sofa for a much needed nap. By the time she woke up, she had an hour before she had to pick up the boys. She put in another load of laundry and had just begun folding the pile of clothes on the sofa when Griffin came through the door.

"You look like I feel," she told him.

"If that's death warmed over, then that would be me."

"I had broth for lunch. Do you want some?"

"That actually doesn't sound bad." He headed for the kitchen.

"It's in a pot on the stove. It might still be warm."

Cassie folded the towel and heard the microwave beep. Moments later Griffin came out carrying a bowl and sat down on the sofa.

"Are you done for the day?"

He swallowed a spoonful of the broth. "I cleared the rest of my schedule."

"Probably not a bad idea. I feel a lot better since I took a nap."

"That's next on my list."

"I'd suggest using the bedroom. The boys will be home in an hour, and it will be a little quieter that way."

"Aren't you going to join me?" There was a hint of the devil in his voice.

Cassie shook her head. "You aren't seriously propositioning me right now, are you?"

"Yes, but whether or not I could perform is another subject altogether."

His comment drew a chuckle from her.

Cassie checked the time. "Gotta go. Take my advice, don't fall asleep here. Use the bedroom."

Griffin nodded, his eyes heavy, and Cassie knew he wouldn't make it to the bed. She tossed a blanket over him. "Your choice. But don't say I didn't warn you."

Griffin set the bowl on the end table and snuggled under the blanket. In moments, he was sound asleep.

Cassie grabbed her purse and headed out to the car. She wished she had the energy to do some grocery shopping and give Griffin a longer nap, but she barely had the strength to pick up the boys and drive home.

When she arrived at the school, she parked next to Sam, who was waiting for Kevin.

Cassie rolled down her window, keeping her distance in case she was still contagious. "Where's Emma?"

"She and Annie are working on some research project she's got going."

Emma was always working on a project. Cassie was beginning to think she loved research more than farming. "So, you're on pickup duty?"

"I am." He studied her closely. "If you don't mind my saying so, you look like hell."

Of course she did. She hadn't put on any makeup this morning, and she hadn't even brushed her hair—just pulled it into a messy ponytail. "You always were a glib devil, Sam Parker."

"Seriously, are you feeling okay?"

"To be frank, no," Cassie said. "The kids gave me the stomach flu this weekend."

Sam took a step back, and she'd bet if he'd had garlic with him he'd have it strung around his neck. "I hate the stomach flu."

Cassie leaned her head back against the seat and let her eyes fall shut. "Join the club."

"Why don't you let me take the boys to the baseball field with

Kevin? I'll bring them home after I'm done there. Or better yet, I'll send them home with Griffin."

"I doubt Griffin will make your meeting today. Last I saw, he was sound asleep on my sofa, recovering from the same affliction I have. He even canceled the rest of his afternoon appointments."

Sam arched a brow at her. "He must be really sick if he did that."

"You think *I* look like hell, double that and you'll get an idea of how Griffin's looking."

Sam cringed and repeated, "There is nothing worse than the stomach flu."

"I agree."

"Go home and take a nap with Griffin. I'll get the boys. "

"Are you sure it's not an imposition?" Cassie only asked out of politeness. She was more than ready to race home and fall into bed.

"I wouldn't have offered if I didn't want to do it."

"Thanks. I owe you."

"How about I bring a pizza for dinner when I come?"

Cassie's stomach rebelled at the mention of food. "Just one for the boys. I'm still on broth, and I don't think Griffin will eat any either." Cassie gave him money, then went home. She dropped her phone and purse on the end table, then went to the bedroom. She found Griffin sprawled on the bed. She curled up beside him. Within seconds she was sound asleep.

THE DOORBELL RANG. Groggy, Griffin looked at the bedside clock and groaned—five o'clock.

"It's probably Sam with the boys," Cassie murmured, her voice still thick with sleep.

"If it was Sam, they would already be inside."

Cassie rolled to her side, pushed herself up off the bed, and headed for the door.

Griffin followed, rubbing sleep from his eyes.

The doorbell rang again as they reached the living room.

Cassie opened the door, and a state trooper stood on the porch.

"Are you Cassandra Cooper?"

Griffin stepped up next to her, and she leaned into him. He slid an arm around her and felt the tension vibrating from her body. "Yes-Yes. Has something happened?"

"I understand you have a cousin, Raymond Donovan, and you're taking care of his children."

"Yes, that's correct. Has something happened to the boys?" Cassie asked in a rush.

"No, this isn't about them. I'm afraid your cousin was found this morning, an apparent overdose. He was rushed to the hospital. I'm terribly sorry, but he died."

Cassie stared at the officer, saying nothing. She kept it together while the officer told her where to collect the body, but Griffin could see she was hanging on by a thread.

As soon as they were alone, Cassie laid her head on Griffin's chest. Her tears warmed his shirt.

"I'm so sorry." He kissed the top of her head then led her into the living room and drew her onto the sofa, holding her while she cried.

"I'm a horrible person," she said, her voice wobbly.

Griffin pushed her hair from her eyes. "Why would you say that?"

"Because there is part of me that's relieved he's gone and there won't be a custody battle."

"That's a natural response. That doesn't mean you're happy he's dead, or that you won't grieve for him."

Cassie released a shaky laugh. "I miss the boy I grew up with. We were close until high school when he started drinking and experimenting with drugs."

Griffin nodded, remembering the lanky kid he'd played sports with all through school. "He was a lot of fun, but he had his demons." His phone vibrated. He glanced at the text. "That was Sam. He's going to pick up the pizza now then bring the boys home."

Cassie shuddered. "How am I going to break this to them?"

The urge to run for the hills pumped adrenaline through Griffin. He didn't want to have to comfort three young boys when they found out

their father was dead. Doing so meant reliving Bobby's death. A dark
hole he didn't want to go down again, but he couldn't walk away from
Cassie or the kids. Instead, he braced himself to confront his own
demons.

Griffin tightened his arms around her. "I'll be with you every step
of the way, and we'll figure it out."

T he funeral was held the following Saturday at First Christian church. Every pew was full to overflowing, and some people even stood outside to remember the boy that they'd all known and loved.

The minister spoke about how Raymond had adored his wife and children. Griffin understood how that kind of grief could tear a man apart. What he couldn't understand was abandoning his children, but he certainly understood loss. He knew it up close and personal, how it could turn a man inside out and make him never want to love again. Fortunately, it had never driven him to drugs and alcohol.

Since Raymond's body was cremated, there was no graveside service. After the funeral, they went to the Beauty Bowl to celebrate his life. A fitting place to celebrate since Raymond spent most of his childhood there.

Griffin watched Tyler as he antagonized his brothers.

Each boy had reacted differently to their father's death—from anger to withdrawal. Griffin didn't know which was easier to handle, but he was beginning to think anger. At least he could relate to that. He understood how the pain made you want to hit someone, something, anything to escape the fury burning inside.

Griffin started to intervene, but fortunately, one of Tyler's friends came over and distracted him, so instead Griffin wandered over to the tables that were set out with food and drink. He poured himself a cup of coffee.

"How are you doing?"

Griffin turned to find Sam beside him.

"It hasn't been easy."

Sam nodded. "We had a lot of good times growing up, didn't we?"

Griffin stared at the bowling lanes where the kids were playing. "We did. We were a lot like our boys over there." He nodded to Jeff and Kevin.

Sam didn't comment on Griffin's slip. They weren't Griffin's boys, but they sure as hell felt like they belonged to him—he wanted to claim them as his.

Was he ready to undertake that responsibility again? Or more to the point, how could he be sure he didn't let them down as he'd done with Mary and Bobby?

"They remind me a lot of us for sure."

"Where's Emma?" Griffin asked, changing the subject.

"In the back changing Annie. She just started crawling, and that girl can get into the biggest mess faster than Kevin does."

Griffin chuckled. "She's going to be a lot like her mama."

"That's what I'm afraid of."

The cowbells clanked, drawing their attention to the door as Chet and Rookie walked in. Chet looked around the room as if searching for a familiar face.

Sam waved him over, and he made a beeline for them.

Chet shook hands with them, then poured himself a cup of coffee. The man's gaze circled the room.

"Cassie's in the back helping Luella," Griffin said, assuming he was looking for his daughter.

"Was I that obvious?"

"Only to those of us in the know."

"How is she doing?"

Griffin shrugged. "About as well as can be expected."

"Here they go again," Sam said.

The boys' roughhousing escalated from fun to anger. Griffin started over to them, but Chet placed a hand on his arm.

"Let me talk to them."

Griffin arched a brow. "Are you sure you want to deal with it?"

"Believe it or not, I actually like kids, and I'm fairly good with them."

Griffin stepped aside and gestured for him to proceed. He and Sam watched Chet and Rookie stroll over and quickly diffuse the situation with some good-natured teasing before challenging them to a foosball game.

"There's nothing like a different adult to make them stand up and take notice," Sam said.

"And don't forget he's Coop, the baseball legend," Griffin reminded him.

Cassie came out of the kitchen and joined them. "Hey, Sam."

Sam nodded at her.

"Where's Emma?" she asked.

"Getting Annie cleaned up."

Cassie smiled. "That girl definitely takes after her mama."

Sam added some cold cuts to his plate. "We were just discussing that."

Emma joined them a moment later with a freshly scrubbed Annie, who was squirming from side to side.

Cassie held out her arms to the baby, and she lunged for her. Cassie hugged her close. "How's my girl?"

Luella came out of the kitchen carrying two heaping platters of food.

"Does Luella need any help?" Griffin asked.

Cassie released an exasperated breath. "I tried to help, but she told me to get out of *her* kitchen. That *she* was handling this."

"Maybe Luella would be more agreeable to male assistance."

Cassie looked up at Griffin, her eyes dark and inscrutable. "She might."

Griffin and Sam went over to talk to Luella.

Emma shook a finger at her. "I'm telling you, that Griffin is a keeper."

Cassie said nothing as she tickled Annie's chin eliciting a giggle. "Yeah, he's one of the good ones," she muttered.

Emma's gaze probed her. "But?"

Cassie shrugged as Annie grabbed a fistful of her hair and wound it around her tiny hand. "But he doesn't talk to me." She carefully removed her hair from Annie's grasp, then rubbed noses with her. "He keeps everything inside."

Emma's eyes darkened with concern. "He's always been that way."

"I know, but I keep feeling like he does all the giving. What do I contribute?" Cassie changed the subject. "There's been a good turnout for Raymond's funeral."

Emma looked as if she had more to say, then shrugged. "Yes."

"Honestly, I wasn't sure how many people would show up," Cassie confessed.

Emma studied the crowd. "They want to remember him as he was, not what he became."

"I do too. I just wish I could give the boys those memories. All they remember is the father who abandoned them."

Emma's gaze moved to Chet where he'd engaged the kids in a foosball tournament. "You can't change the past, Cassie. It's amazing how resilient kids are. Look at Kevin."

Cassie watched at the children laughing and playing. "Kevin had you and Sam to give him plenty of love and attention."

"And Jeff, Tyler, and Trevor have you."

Would she be enough?

Emma wrapped an arm around her shoulder. "You're there for them and so is the rest of the community." Emma nodded at Chet. "Look at your dad. He's working hard to become part of their lives."

Annie began to fuss, and as Cassie handed her back to Emma, she saw Chet high-five one of the boys. Deep down she wanted him to be the father and grandfather that she could turn to when she needed love and support.

GRIFFIN DROVE Cassie and the boys home after helping Aunt Luella clean up. Jeff fell asleep, and Trevor and Tyler stared out the window.

Tyler broke the silence. "Now that dad's dead, does that mean we're going to live with you forever?"

Cassie turned to look at him. "You'll be staying with me. We're a family now."

"All of us—Griffin, too?"

Cassie opened her mouth to respond, but Griffin answered for her. "I'll always be here for you guys—*always.*"

Griffin's reassurance seemed to satisfy Tyler, and he said nothing more the rest of the ride home, but his words troubled her. He'd only stressed he'd be there for the kids. To what degree, he hadn't said. In fact, there was a lot he hadn't elaborated on, and it left Cassie wondering where she stood with him.

Griffin parked in the driveway, and he carried Jeff inside to his room.

"You boys go shower and get ready for bed," Cassie said. Neither objected, which was a first. They always wanted to stay up later, especially on the weekend.

Cassie went into the kitchen, saw the boxes that held Raymond's belongings sitting on the table. She lifted the lid and found pictures of the boys on top and underneath a letter addressed to her. She opened it.

Cassie:

I'm sorry for all the things I said. Giving up the boys was harder than I thought it would be. But I can see now you were right. They need stability. They need a parent—something I can't be for them. I wish I were stronger. Tell them I love them. Don't let them forget me.

Raymond.

A tear slid down Cassie's cheek and onto the paper. She quickly folded it and put it back in the envelope. She would do everything in her power to make sure the boys never forgot their father.

GRIFFIN FOUND Cassie sitting at the table. He rested his hands on her shoulders. "Do you need help going through this?"

She shook her head. "I didn't intend to do this tonight. I was just looking at some of the things, and I came across this."

She handed him the letter.

Griffin opened it, read it, then put it back in the envelope. "He really did want what was best for them."

Cassie nodded, her fingers repeatedly pleating the tablecloth. "I wish it could've been different."

"Me, too."

"It's been a long day. Let's go to bed and deal with this tomorrow."

Cassie followed him into the bedroom and went into the bathroom. Griffin undressed then stared out the window. Nothing but total blackness other than the neighbor's porch light down the road.

Why had he managed to continue functioning after Bobby died, but Raymond had fallen apart after losing Marie? Not that he'd come through Bobby's death unscathed. At first, he'd shut down and compartmentalized his emotions—those he could deal with and those he couldn't. And he still had a fair amount he couldn't deal with.

Cassie pressed her cheek to his back and slid her arms around him. "What are you thinking about?"

She had enough on her plate without taking on his baggage. He turned and kissed her. "Just remembering the good times with Raymond."

A partial truth. He'd been thinking about Raymond, but he couldn't talk to her about Bobby. If he did, he'd lose control of his emotions and end up like Raymond—a broken, empty man.

22

The Sunday after the funeral, Griffin breezed into the kitchen a bag of baseball equipment slung over his shoulder as Cassie took a plate from the cupboard.

"Going somewhere?" she asked.

"Yeah, to throw some balls for the boys before it gets dark."

A misty rain trickled past the window as she set crackers and cheese on the plate. "Not ideal weather for baseball."

Griffin shrugged. "A little rain never hurt anyone."

True, but she preferred wine and cheese by the fire.

"Come on, guys. Let's get a move on," he called out.

Trevor, the most diehard player of the three shouted from the family room, "I changed my mind. I don't wanna go."

"Jeff, Tyler," Griffin shouted.

Tyler poked his head through the doorway. "Me and Jeff are gonna play a game instead," he said, then raced back down the hall to their bedroom.

Cassie rolled her eyes as their bickering floated back.

"I wanna play a video game," Jeff whined.

"No, we're playing—" Tyler's voice faded away as the bedroom door slammed shut.

Cassie removed the cork from a bottle of wine. "Looks like you've been stood up."

Griffin dropped the bag. "I'll get them to change their minds."

Filling two glasses, she handed them to him while she grabbed the plate. "How about we take advantage of some quiet time in front of the fire?"

He hesitated, then shrugged and followed her into the living room.

The glow of the fire lent a cozy feel to the room as Cassie set the platter on the coffee table and settled onto the sofa. She patted the seat beside her. Griffin sat down next her, handing her a glass of wine.

Tucking her feet underneath her, she cuddled into him. "This is nice."

The mist turned to a steady rainfall that Cassie found soothing.

"Did I tell you I joined a single mother's group and a parenting group on Facebook?"

"No, you didn't."

"Must have slipped my mind with all that's been going on. Anyway they've suggested some great books and articles I've been reading."

Griffin placed a slice of cheese on a cracker and settled back onto the sofa. "About what?"

"A lot of it has been about the importance of unstructured play and making sure kids are given time to be kids. It's made me realize how fortunate I was to have the childhood I did, and I want the boys to have time to just play with their friends, to be bored and learn how to fill that time."

Griffin stared into the fire. "I never had that kind of freedom. Dad felt it was important to keep me and my brothers busy. Our days went from one activity to the next."

Cassie nibbled on a piece of cheese. "I remember, but you also spent a lot of time playing with Sam, Ryan, Emma, and me."

His voice turned wistful. "Only because Mom insisted. She said kids needed time to just play without adults interfering. I heard her and Dad arguing about it several times, but Mom won out, mostly because Dad was never home."

Cassie tilted her head to study him. "That must have been hard."

Griffin nodded. "It was."

"I wonder why he felt so driven to fill every moment with activity?"

Griffin sipped his wine. "Just part of his personality I suppose."

She swirled her wine. "It's easy to pattern after our parents."

"How so?"

"Mom used to make empty promises to me all the time, and I've caught myself about to do the same with the kids."

"Why?"

Cassie mulled over his question. "They've been through so much I want to protect them from disappointment, heartache, and loss. Raymond's death has made me realize I can't do that. They need to grieve, to process what's happened. All I can do is be there for them the same as you've done for me since the kids arrived. Whenever I found myself floundering, you've been there to encourage and support me."

The thump of Griffin's heart sounded in her ear, reassuring and comforting as he stroked her hair. "It's been my pleasure."

She leaned into him. "You've been my rock since I found out about Mom's death, then Raymond's." She tilted her head to look up at him. "Let me be there for you. I know you cared about Raymond. I know you're hurting inside," she hesitated, then continued. "I know the anniversary of Bobby's death is next week."

His hand stilled. "I appreciate the offer, but I'm good."

His immediate rejection left her hollow inside. Why couldn't he share his pain with her?

She studied his expression. "I love you and I know that you love me, but this is the intimacy I told you I wanted when we first started dating. Whenever the discussion involves emotions you go into doctor mode."

"Doctor mode?"

His calm, neutral tone annoyed her. "It's the term I use for how you handle an emergency. You push your feelings down and focus on everyone but yourself just like you're doing now."

"And that's a bad thing?"

"Not in a medical emergency, but it is when you use it to shut me out. In that regard, you're a lot like your father. He taught you how to be a dedicated, caring physician, but at the expense of your own needs."

Griffin shoved to his feet and paced the room, then stopped, facing her. "I'm not my father—not since Bobby died. I made a promise to myself I would be there for the people I love. Haven't I been there for you and the boys?" he demanded.

Cassie remained calm in the face of his outburst, recognizing that his anger covered his real feelings. "Yes, you have, but that's not the issue, Griffin."

"What is?"

"Our one-sided relationship. You're here physically, but emotionally you're detached, and your time is always filled. Is that to avoid your grief?"

His nostrils flared. "What do you want from me?"

She rose and he took another step back, retreating further from her physically and emotionally, but Cassie held her ground. "Some honest emotion."

"Okay, fine. I'm sad that Raymond is dead, and I wish he'd gone into rehab so he could be here for his kids."

"And?"

"And what?"

Her temper flared. "You're still in doctor mode. Telling me what I want to hear in that calm, unemotional tone, but you're still holding in your true feelings. Why can't you let me comfort you?"

His anguish filled the room. "Because I'm terrified that if I do, I'll end up like Raymond, looking for the next high to get me through the day."

Her gaze locked with his. "Avoidance takes on many forms. Raymond chose drugs and alcohol. You're choosing to deal with yours alone. Neither one works for me."

Cassie walked out, her chest aching because she was afraid Griffin wouldn't be able to become the man she needed him to be.

CASSIE GOT the kids to school the next morning, then headed to Sittin'
Pretty to do some deep cleaning and sort out her problems with Griffin.
He'd been unusually quiet since their argument the night before, and
she didn't know what he was feeling. And that, in a nutshell, was the
problem. He wouldn't talk to her about it.

Cassie attacked the room taking out her frustrations scrubbing, ster-
ilizing, and sweeping. By one o'clock, Sittin' Pretty gleamed, her frustrations with Griffin spent, and her stomach demanding food.

She went to the restaurant and into the kitchen where her aunt had a
line of burgers frying. Cassie slipped on an apron and began helping
her.

"I thought Laverne was filling in today?" she said to Luella.

"Sick as a dog."

"Why didn't you call me? I could've come and helped earlier."

"It's your day off, and I knew you were busy cleaning."

"I could've done that later."

Aunt Luella shrugged. "I managed. Besides, I'm through the lunch
rush now, and as soon as we finish up these orders, we can have lunch
together."

Cassie carried out the orders and refilled coffee cups and water
glasses. A half hour later, the restaurant was virtually empty. She went
back to the kitchen and found her aunt fixing their burgers. Cassie
poured them each a cup of coffee and carried them out to the table in
the far corner, away from prying eyes but in line with the cash register.
Moments later, her aunt hustled out with their food.

They sat down and began eating.

"So, how are the boys doing?" Aunt Luella asked.

Cassie shrugged. "Depends on which boy you're asking about.
They're all dealing with Raymond's death differently. Jeff cries himself
to sleep at night. Tyler acts like nothing's happened, and Trevor is
angry." She sensed Trevor's anger stemmed from something more than
his father's death.

Her aunt reached for the bottle of ketchup. "Tyler is the one I'd worry about."

"Why?"

"Because the other two are at least showing some emotion. Tyler needs to release that grief he's got all bottled up inside of him before he goes off like a powder keg or develops an ulcer."

Just like Griffin. "What do you suggest? Bowling? Baseball? The Bible?"

She shook a finger at Cassie. "There's nothing wrong with the three B's. They're all good for the soul."

Cassie smiled for what felt like the first time in weeks. "I wasn't criticizing, I was asking your opinion."

Her aunt took a bite of her burger as she considered the question. "I always found the best way with you was to talk while you fixed my hair. You always seemed to open up more when your hands were occupied. And don't forget, I only had you. With three, you've got the oldest, youngest, and the middle child to contend with, and middle children tend to get ignored. Not intentional, just the way things happen. I was a middle child, and I remember feeling that way. Get a little one-on-one time alone with Tyler. Take him for a walk. Play one of those confounded video games the kids love nowadays, or just take him for an ice cream cone and see what happens."

Her aunt always had a wealth of good old-fashioned common sense. Cassie reached over and squeezed her hand. "Thank you."

"For what?"

"For taking me in. For being the mother mine couldn't be. For always being there for me. Mostly, thank you for being in my life."

"That goes double for me." Her aunt's voice turned wistful. "I wish I could have done the same for Raymond." She took a napkin from the holder and dabbed her eyes. "I should have done more."

"I think you need to take your own advice."

"How so?"

"Forgive yourself. You did everything possible for him."

Aunt Luella released a noisy sigh. "You're right. I just wish we could've found a way to save him."

"Me, too," Cassie whispered. "Me, too." She reached into her purse and took out the letter he'd left her. She handed it to her aunt.

Aunt Luella opened the envelope and scanned the sheet of paper. "So, with this letter, does that mean you'll be able to keep custody of the boys?"

"I haven't talked to the attorney yet, but I suspect so."

"When will you see him again?"

"I have to make an appointment for Thursday. I'd really like to get this settled so that the boys know they won't be uprooted. I think if anything good can come of Raymond's death, it would be that they have stability back in their lives."

"If you need me to watch them, I'll be here."

"Thank you. I can always count on you."

Her aunt's watery gaze held hers. "Always."

23

A week later, Griffin closed the office and went home without a word to anyone, including Cassie. He parked in the garage, and his phone rang as he stepped inside the house.

Glancing at the screen, he groaned—his mother. He wanted to avoid her, especially today, but he answered it. "Hi Mom. How's Herb?"

"He's fine. How are you?"

His gaze landed on the photo of his son on the mantle. "I'm fine."

"Really? Where are you?

"Home."

"Alone?"

"Yes."

Silence, broken by her breathing. "Why are you home alone instead of with Cassie and the boys?"

"I don't want to burden them with this."

Her mother made a tsking sound. "This is what family is for. You lean on them. What if Cassie were going through something like this? What would you do on a day like today?"

Without thinking he said, "I'd comfort her."

"And don't you think she wants to do the same for you?"

He knew she did, but he couldn't let her do that. He didn't deserve it. "You don't understand." His gaze remained locked on the photo. Bobby would be four if he'd lived, but he would forever be a two-year-old in Griffin's mind.

"I understand perfectly. You were Bobby's father. It was your job to protect him. You don't want anyone to ease your guilt because you don't feel deserving of forgiveness. Is that on target?"

Griffin said nothing.

"Your father had many fine qualities, but teaching you how control your emotions was not one of them. It's not healthy, and as a physician, you know that. Look at what it did to him. Dead of a heart attack at fifty-five. If you don't share this with Cassie sooner or later you will lose her. Is that what you want?"

His mother disconnected the call, leaving him alone with his memories.

～

"Why isn't Griffin tucking me in?"

Cassie had called Griffin several times today, but every call had gone straight to voicemail. He'd chosen to deal with the anniversary of his son's death alone. It told her what she'd known for some time—he didn't love her enough to share the most painful parts of his past. She'd known it last week when she'd tried to talk to him about Raymond. This was proof positive he chose to go it on his own.

She sat down on Jeff's bed, smoothing the hair from his forehead. "He's at his house," she said, deciding honesty was the best route.

Jeff's eyes went round. "This is his house. Why isn't he here?"

Of course Jeff thought that. Griffin had spent almost every night here for the last two months. Now that she thought about it, he'd only put a few things in the closet and dresser, but everything personal remained at his place.

"He just needed some time alone today."

Jeff tilted his head to look up at her. "Did you have a fight?"

How could they fight when he wasn't here? "No."

"Is he mad at us 'cause we were fighting?"

Cassie scooped him into her arms and hugged him close. "No, absolutely not."

"Then call him and tell him to come home. I miss him."

Jeff's words tore at her, but she didn't call Griffin. For now she'd give him space and wait for him to come to her.

CASSIE WAITED two days for Griffin to reach out to her, but not a phone call or a text. Finally, she'd had enough and she was through waiting for him to come out of hibernation. If he wouldn't come to her, she was going to see him and have it out with him once and for all.

Her eleven o'clock appointment cancelled, so she grabbed her purse and headed over to Griffin's office. She parked next to his truck and went inside.

Cassie paused long enough to say to his receptionist, "Tell Griffin I'll be waiting for him in his office," then breezed down the hall, finding his office door open. She went inside to wait, and she would stay here until he talked to her.

Moments later she heard the low murmur of his voice as he conversed with his receptionist, then he entered the office and closed the door.

"I have patients waiting."

"Then maybe you shouldn't have ducked my calls for the last two days."

A red flush stained his cheeks and neck. "I've had some things to take care of."

"You've been mourning—alone."

He released a weary breath. "Is it wrong to need a little time alone?"

She softened her tone. "No, it's not. What's wrong is shutting me out. I love you, Griffin. I want to share my life with you, but you do all the giving."

He stepped up to her. "I love you, too."

"I know you do."

"Then what's the problem?"

She took his hand. "Plenty of people love each other, but their relationships fail. Do you know why?"

Silence.

"Because it's a one-way relationship. One person does all the heavy lifting. But what's worse is it's lonely to be left out. I know you're hurting and you won't let me comfort you. That hurts."

"There's nothing you can do."

"Maybe, but think about how you'd feel if I hadn't shared about my mother."

"That's different."

Cassie studied him. "Different because it would be happening to you and not me. I want to build a life with you, but only if we are a couple who shares everything."

She kissed him, then grabbed her purse and walked out. The choice was his. He either came to her because he wanted a life with her, or he didn't.

CASSIE LOCKED up and headed for home the next evening. Chet had offered to pick up the boys from practice. She'd accepted, grateful for the help since Griffin was still MIA after she spoke with him the day before. She was trying to convince herself his silence meant it was over between them, but she kept hoping he'd come to her.

Why hadn't Griffin fought for her?

Was that what she expected? To have him prove his love by sharing himself?

Yes.

She got into her car and drove home. The house was dark when she pulled up. She'd become accustomed to Griffin arriving first and starting dinner.

Her phone buzzed as she entered the kitchen. She looked down to see a text from Chet.

Bringing dinner. Don't bother cooking.

The tension in Cassie's shoulders eased. The man could be pretty damn thoughtful. He texted again.

Put your feet up. Have a glass of wine.

She texted back.

THX.

Chet and the boys arrived a half hour later.

The kids wolfed down the pizza, talking a mile a minute and arguing good-naturedly for once. When they were done, they cleaned up their mess without a word and went into the living room, leaving her alone with Chet.

He collected their dishes then took her coat from the hook next to the door. "Walk with me."

She glanced out the dark window. "I'm beat. Could we do it another time?"

"Please. Just a short walk. Trevor can handle things for twenty minutes, and Rookie will be here with them." He held out her coat for her. "Trevor," he called into the next room. "Your mom and I are going for a walk. You're in charge until we get back."

Trevor waved in acknowledgement, not looking up from the video game he was playing with Tyler.

Chet had her out the door before she could offer up another protest. She shivered and zipped her coat, then tugged on the gloves he handed her.

"It's freezing out here," she grumbled.

"Then we'd best keep moving." He took her arm and started walking. "I had lunch with Luella this afternoon, and she told me Griffin was staying at his house."

Great, just what she needed. Her aunt telling everyone about her love life.

They reached the end of the drive, and Chet sat down on the bench she'd put there for decoration. He patted the wooden seat beside him.

She glanced at the house where smoke curled out of the chimney. "We could be inside where it's warm instead of out here in the cold."

"There are too many listening ears inside." He patted the seat again.

Resigned, she sat so he would say whatever was on his mind, then they could go back to the house.

Chet stared up at the full moon shining down on them, so bright she could easily make out his features. "You realize he loves you."

She did not want to discuss Griffin. Her tone came out more clipped than she'd intended. "I do. His love isn't at question."

She flinched when Chet laid an arm over her shoulder. "If love isn't the problem, is he bad in bed?"

"No!"

Her father's blue eyes crinkled with amusement. "Then why?"

"I don't want to discuss this."

His arm tightened around her. "Talk to me. I want to help."

The man was as bad as Aunt Luella about butting into her life, but wasn't this exactly what she'd accused Griffin of doing? Keeping his emotions bottled up inside.

"Tuesday was the anniversary of his son's death. He wouldn't return my calls or texts, so I went to his office and told him that for our relationship to work I expected more."

Shaking his head, Chet looked up at the sky as if searching for guidance. "Let me guess. He's doing all the giving except when it comes to talking about his son."

"Yes."

"Sharing doesn't come naturally for most men."

"So, you're saying I should just accept his behavior?"

"Hell no. You need to fight for what you want, what you deserve."

His words struck a chord deep within her.

"So, what are you going to do now?" he asked.

"I don't know. I've told Griffin what I want, so it's up to him."

Chet hugged her close and pressed a kiss to her hair. "I'm here for you whenever you need me."

He started to rise, but she caught his hand first. "There is something you could do for me."

"Name it."

"Could you take the boys to school tomorrow and pick them up after? I need to go to Chicago to see the attorney."

"Sure, I'd love to."

Cassie shivered. "Let's go back and get something warm to drink."

They discussed her trip to Chicago over tea, then Chet glanced at his watch. "Time for me to head home."

Cassie followed him to the living room where Rookie lay on the floor between Tyler and Jeff. "Gotta go, boys. See you tomorrow."

Jeff ran over and threw his arms around him. "See you tomorrow, Chet."

Her father hugged him back, and she saw a sheen of tears in his eyes. He straightened, and it was gone.

Cassie walked him to the door. She raised up on tiptoe and kissed his cheek. "Thanks again for taking care of the boys tomorrow."

He glanced at them, then back at her. "I should be thanking you."

She watched as he and Rookie followed the sidewalk to his truck. The more time she spent with Chet, the more confident she felt trusting him. He'd been open and honest with her, and right now, he was the only man she could count on.

24

For the last week Griffin had gone to his house instead of Cassie's, and it left an emptiness inside reminiscent of the days after Bobby died.

Griffin went to work and came home every night, *alone*. His house had no children, no laughter, no chaos, no fights. Oh, he'd admit to wishing for a quiet moment to himself occasionally, but then he remembered his life since Bobby died.

Solitude was highly overrated.

But it wasn't just the boys that he sought out—it was Cassie. The woman had gotten under his skin. When the boys arrived, she'd been overwhelmed with the responsibilities of instant parenthood and leaned on him, but their relationship had evolved, changing from childhood friends to lovers.

Her eyes had always drawn him, sparkling with laughter, the hint of the devil when playful, and buried sorrow that spoke of abandonment. There was so much more to the woman than a beautiful face and body he could spend a lifetime exploring. He wanted to know every facet of her.

Griffin left the office for his meeting with Chet and Sam at Cornhusker field.

Chet always arrived early, and he was there when Griffin walked through the door. Rookie rushed over to greet him, his tail wagging furiously.

"You look like hell," Chet said.

Griffin scowled at him as he petted Rookie then poured himself a cup of coffee. "Thanks for not *sugarcoating* it."

"In case you haven't realized it yet, I tell it like I see it."

Griffin appreciated that about the man.

"So, do you want to talk about it?"

Griffin stood at the window and stared out at the barren baseball field, snowflakes drifting from the sky. "There's nothing to talk about?"

Chet shook his head. "You're just as stubborn as my daughter," he muttered. "In the short time I've been here, I've learned some things about Cassie. She is a lot like me whether she'll admit it or not. She tells it like it is, and I suspect that's what she did with you." He paused a beat, the continued. "I'm guessing you didn't like what she had to say."

Griffin didn't deny his assertion since it was spot on.

Sam entered, and Rookie rushed over to him. Squatting down, he rubbed his ears, then poured himself a cup of coffee before looking at Griffin. "You look like hell."

"So I've been told. Can we skip the chitchat and get on with the meeting?"

"Someone's moody today."

Griffin scowled at his friend but chose not to react to the bait. "What's on the agenda?"

He watched as Sam and Chet debated whether to press him further, then finally Sam opened the folder he'd laid on the table, and the meeting began, much to Griffin's relief. They went over potential prospects for next season.

Sam's phone buzzed as they were wrapping up. He stepped out to answer it.

Griffin poured himself another cup of coffee.

"Cassie's going out of town, and I'm going to be watching the boys for a few days."

"She asked you to watch them?"

Chet's eyes narrowed. "Why not me?"

"I'm just surprised, that's all." Griffin said. "Where's she going?"

"You'll have to ask her."

Sam came back into the room, ending their discussion, but somehow Griffin got the impression that was fine with Chet. He'd dropped that bombshell intentionally. He'd wanted Griffin to know Cassie was leaving town, then he'd driven the knife deeper by telling him she'd left the boys with him rather than ask Griffin to watch them.

She was moving on without him. Maybe the best thing for her was if he did nothing. She needed a whole man, not a damaged one.

If that was the right thing to do, why did he feel compelled to go after her?

GRIFFIN LEFT the ballpark and went to the hospital to do a routine surgery on a Cornhusker player. He came out of surgery several hours later to find Trevor had texted him, immediately taking him back to the day Bobby died and Mary's texts.

He shook off the memory and read Trevor's text.

Going to help Katy. She's being picked on. A red-faced scowling emoji.

Where are you?

The park on South Street.

Why hadn't Trevor said something sooner? Maybe he would have if Griffin hadn't locked himself away from Cassie and the kids.

Griffin dialed Trevor's phone. It went to voicemail.

He disconnected the call and texted as he left the doctor's lounge.

Was in surgery. Headed home.

Don't bother. Handling it.

What the hell did that mean? How was he handling it? All the things he'd heard on the news about kids being bullied left him uneasy. Was Trevor putting himself in danger?

Handling it how?

No answer.

Griffin pushed out of the glass double doors and headed to his truck.

His phone dinged.

Pick me up and I'll tell you about it.

Where?

Trevor sent him his location.

Minutes later Griffin turned onto Third Street, and Trevor was waiting on the corner for him. He pulled alongside the sidewalk.

Trevor trotted up to the pickup. "Hey Griffin, what's up?"

He climbed into the truck and Griffin asked, "Spill. What happened?"

A huge grin engulfed his face. "There were some guys at school that have been picking on Katy, so I walked her home. They followed us, and I told them to leave or I was calling the cops."

"And that worked?"

"Nah. They just laughed at me."

"So what did you do?"

"I showed them the video Connor took of them at school bullying Katy. I told them I was going to show it to the cops unless they left her alone."

"So did they?"

A self-satisfied grin covered his face. "Yup. They ran off before the video even finished playing."

Griffin clapped him on the back. "An excellent plan. I'm proud of you."

Trevor's smile dimmed. "I'm not going to be like my dad."

"What do you mean?"

"He ran away from me, and Tyler, and Jeff. I'm not going to do that. Even if it hurts, I'm going to face my fears. Dad didn't do that, and I don't respect that."

The kid was wise beyond his twelve years. Griffin understood why

Trevor felt as he did, but he didn't totally agree. "Some people are so damaged it's hard for them to look beyond the present to the future."

"You think Dad was like that?"

"I do."

Trevor thought over his comment. "Dad turned to drugs when Mom died, but you didn't do that when your son died, did you?"

Griffin stared out the windshield, thinking of Raymond and how easy it would have been to drink himself into oblivion after he lost Bobby. He hadn't handled his grief a whole lot better. "I buried myself in my work. That's not an ideal way to handle it either."

"At least you were helping people. What did Dad do?" Trevor demanded.

"Just because your dad turned to drugs doesn't mean he didn't love you and your brothers. I think he gave you guys to Cassie because he knew she would love and care for you. And that's what happened, right?"

Trevor shrugged. "I guess, but I think you're making excuses for him."

"Maybe partially, but hanging on to anger only hurts you and I don't want you to do that," Griffin said.

Trevor said nothing in response.

Griffin put the truck in gear and headed for the Beauty Bowl.

"You sounded funny when you called. Was something wrong?"

Griffin stared out the windshield. His first reaction was to just give a lame excuse, but Trevor deserved the truth. "When I came out of surgery, I saw your text and it reminded me of when my son died."

"How?"

"I didn't spend a lot of time with Bobby when he was alive. I worked all the time. The day Bobby died, I scheduled a surgery rather than be with him and my wife. I didn't have to do it, but his mom and I had been fighting and I didn't want to deal with it. My wife had been texting me just like you did."

Griffin pulled into the Beauty Bowl and parked, then faced Trevor. "As I was finishing the surgery, a nurse came in to tell me they'd been in an accident. If I'd have gone with them, I might have been able to save Bobby, at the very least have seen him before he died, but instead I avoided my wife and the problems we were having. I took the coward's way out."

Trevor studied him a long moment. "Did Bobby know you loved him?"

"Yes."

"Do you know for sure if you'd been there you could have saved him?"

"No."

"Then I think you need to stop blaming yourself. You did the best you could."

"Sometimes that's easier said than done. It was my job as a father to keep my son safe. I failed."

Trevor's dark gaze probed his. "So, what you're saying is even though you did the best you could, it's still your fault, but you're also forgiving my dad for being weak. That's lame."

Trevor's words struck a chord deep inside of him. This constant blame ate away at him, and impacted not only him, but Cassie and the boys.

It was time he was as honest with Cassie as she'd been with him. He just hoped he hadn't waited too long.

2 5

Cassie finished packing early Wednesday morning for the convention in Coeur d'Alene, Idaho. She'd signed up for it last August, and after that she'd planned to head to Paradise Falls for a couple of days to meet up with her cousins. It wasn't the ideal time to leave, but she needed to go and try out new products and learn new techniques. When she'd signed up, Aunt Luella had offered to watch the boys, but she was short-handed at the Beauty Bowl and taking on the boys was too much whether she'd admit it or not. And Emma and Sam had plans, so she'd debating cancelling until Chet offered to stay with them.

Jeff burst into her room, bouncing up and down with excitement. "Are Chet and Rookie really going to stay with us while you're gone?"

Cassie sat down on the bed. "Yes."

"Yippee!"

"I'll only be a phone call away if you need to talk to me."

Jeff's expression turned serious. "I'm going to miss you."

Cassie squeezed him and kissed the top of his head. "I'm going to miss you, too, but I'll only be gone a few days."

"I'll be okay," Jeff assured her.

"I know you will. Chet will keep you guys so busy you won't know that I'm gone. You'll have lots of fun."

Jeff nodded against her chest. "We will."

The doorbell rang.

Jeff shoved away. "That's Chet." His footsteps thudded down the hall.

Cassie rose and followed him, her doubts resurfacing about leaving them with Chet until she found all three boys circled around her dad, jumping up and down. Rookie's tail wagged in obvious delight. The kids were clearly excited to be spending a few days with Chet, and he was equally pleased to be spending time with them. He wanted to be part of her family, and maybe it was time she admitted the truth. She wanted her father in her life.

"Close the door, boys. You're letting in the cold air, and Chet's probably freezing," Cassie said.

Chet looked up at her, his eyes crinkling with what Cassie could only term as unadulterated joy. "I can't tell you how much I've been looking forward to this time with them."

The sincerity in his voice left a warm feeling inside of her. "And I'm grateful for the help."

"Have you finished packing?" he asked.

"Not yet. I was working on it when you arrived."

"Go, I've got this. We're going to have fun, aren't we, boys?"

"We are," they yelled in chorus.

Cassie cast a dubious glance at Chet. "You're sure you can handle this?"

Chet rolled his eyes and gave her a nudge toward the bedroom. "I've dealt with up and coming baseball players that were rowdier than these three. We're going to be fine. Now go get ready while I get these guys to school."

Cassie watched the four of them together for a moment, then went to finish packing confident leaving her father in charge was the right thing to do.

~

Cassie attended seminars on coloring, hair styling for special events, and tested new straightening and coloring products. By Saturday morning she was exhausted and ready to head home the next day. Staring out her hotel room window at Lake Coeur d'Alene, she wished Griffin was here with her.

Stop it!

He'd made his decision, and it didn't include her. Time to move on.

She watched the boats bobbing on the water and considered cancelling her trip to Paradise Falls, then nixed that idea. C.J and Maggie would be furious with her if she did, and it was only be a little over an hour up there.

Why not? Chet had urged her to take some time for herself.

Taking out her phone, she set up a rental car. An hour later, she was on the road headed north to Paradise Falls.

Saturday morning Griffin drove to Cassie's house.

Tyler opened the door and let out a whoop. "Griffin's here." He threw his arms around him. "I've missed you."

Griffin hugged Tyler tight against him. Why had he stayed away? He'd done it without considering how it would impact the kids, and on the heels of losing their dad. They needed him, and he would make it up to them.

Jeff and Trevor came racing to the door. "Griffin," they shouted, throwing themselves at him.

He hugged all three boys at once. "I've missed you guys."

"We've been right here," Jeff said, with wide-eyed innocence. "You could've seen us any time."

Again, his fault. He'd only considered his wants and needs when he stayed away.

"You're right, I could have. I'm sorry."

Trevor studied him, his eyes solemn, his expression closed. "We missed you," he said.

Griffin wrapped an arm around his shoulder and squeezed him

tighter. Trevor resisted, then melted into him. "I'm going to fix this, I promise," he whispered around the emotion knotted in his throat. "Where's Chet?"

"Doing the dishes," Jeff said. Taking his hand, he pulled toward the kitchen.

Chet looked up from wiping the counter and offered Griffin a cup of coffee.

"He can't. He's going to make up with Cassie." Trevor gave Griffin a long look that said he'd darn well better be planning on doing that.

Chet's keen gaze studied Griffin, then Trevor. "I didn't know you were going to Idaho."

"I didn't either until just now."

"You're going to the beauty conference, too?" Jeff asked.

"I am," Griffin said.

Chet hid a smile. "You didn't hear that from me."

"My lips are sealed. I've just got to book a flight."

"I might just have access to a private jet."

Griffin studied the older man subtly playing cupid the same as Trevor. "I don't want using the jet to cause problems between you and Cassie."

Chet's blue gaze, so like Cassie's, studied him. "I don't see how ensuring her happiness could upset her."

"You're assuming that she'll be happy about my arrival."

Chet shrugged. "I want to be on good terms with her, but that doesn't mean that I totally agree with her."

"How soon before the jet will be ready?"

Chet's eyes twinkled with unsuppressed glee. "I'd say it'll be ready in about an hour, but you'll be flying straight to Paradise Falls instead of Coeur d'Alene."

"Why?"

"Cassie called earlier, and she's driving up to Paradise Falls to see her cousins for a couple of days."

"Is that really the best time for me to show up?"

He was silent a moment, then said, "Stop procrastinating and go get your girl."

Griffin told the boys goodbye and promised to be back soon. Thirty minutes later, he was on a private jet that would take him to the woman he loved. He just hoped she'd give him a second chance.

CASSIE PARKED at Pulaski's Bar and Grill mid-morning. She entered the massive wood door and went to the kitchen to find her uncle, Charlie Pulaski, removing French bread from the oven while his brother-in-law and partner, Erwin Stein chopped vegetables. Both men were well into their sixties and never seemed to slow down.

"Uncle Charlie?"

He rinsed his hands and dried them on the towel tucked into his apron, then enveloped her in a bear hug. "You made it." He studied her closely. "Erwin, don't you think she looks more and more Amber Rose?"

Erwin took a pair of glasses from his pocket and put them on to study her. "As if she'd rose from the dead."

Charlie pulled a stool up to the counter and gestured for her to sit down. "Coffee?" he asked, pouring a cup before she responded.

Cassie wrapped her hands around the mug while he poured some for him and Erwin. He sat on the stool across from her, and Erwin joined them.

"So how are the boys doing?" Charlie asked.

A swell of emotion filled her, the same as it did whenever she was reminded of Raymond. "It's been hard on them losing their dad."

"How could it not?" Erwin asked. "Raymond had his demons, but he loved those boys."

Charlie nodded in agreement.

Cassie squeezed their hands. "He did, didn't he?"

"Absolutely," they said in unison.

The rear door opened, Genevieve McVey Yang, the sixty-something proprietor of Ye Olde Hardware store entered.

"Genevieve, about time you got here," Charlie boomed.

The hint of some flowery perfume wafted as Genevieve came over and hugged Cassie.

"It's so good to see you," Cassie said. "And before I forget, Aunt Luella said to tell you she's planning to come up after the holidays."

Erwin gave Genevieve his stool while Charlie poured her a cup of coffee.

Genevieve clapped her hands. "Perfect. She'll be here to help us with our latest *project*."

Cassie would bet Luella planned her trip to coincide with Uncle Charlie's Trench Coat Brigade or TCB *project*. The group always had a mystery to solve, and its members included: Charlie, Erwin, Genevieve, and her granddaughter, Becca.

Before they could drag her into their latest whodunit, her cousin C.J. arrived and rescued her. She shook a finger at Charlie. "Dad, you promised you wouldn't pester Cassie about the TCB *project*."

Charlie held up his hands in mock innocence. "We were only discussing that Luella would be coming after to Christmas to help us."

C.J.'s gaze circled the group. "Okay, but no TCB talk while Cassie is here." She grabbed a slice of bread from the counter, then linked arms with Cassie. "I'm starving. Maggie's waiting for us at Brother Murphy's."

Cassie waved goodbye to the group, but before they left, Charlie called out, "Wait." He crossed over to the desk in the corner and rummaged through the drawer, coming back with a key. "You'll need this to get into the cabin."

The lakefront *cabin* was more of a mansion to Cassie's way of thinking that Charlie kept for family to use. "Thank you." Cassie hugged her uncle, then followed C.J. into the dining room, anxious to spend time with her cousins and forget about her breakup with Griffin.

Cassie, C.J., and Maggie sat at a secluded table at Brother Murphy's. Liam, Maggie's brother, owned the pub and had saved the table for them.

Once they were seated, Maggie squeezed her hand. "I was so sorry to hear about your mom." She reached into her purse and handed her a photo. "Mom sent this. She thought you might like to have it."

Tears rushed to Cassie's eyes when she saw the photo of her mom taken before the drugs and alcohol ravished her body.

Tracing a finger over the beautiful blonde with sparkling blue eyes swinging Cassie high into the air, she felt a tug of longing. She wanted that woman back.

Cassie fingered her mother's necklace and wondered what her life would have been like if her mother had told Chet the truth.

Water under the bridge. It didn't make any difference now, and there was no point in dwelling on the past.

She blinked back more tears, pressing the photo to her chest before putting it in her purse. "Thank her for me."

"So, what's going on with you and Griffin?" C.J. demanded in her take no prisoner's voice.

Cassie's gaze swept over her cousin. "How did you know about Griffin?"

Maggie rolled her eyes. "Aunt Luella, who else?"

"You talked to her?" Cassie asked.

Maggie shook her head. "No, Mom did. Quit stalling and tell us what happened between you two?"

Cassie sipped her tea to bolster herself before spilling the whole story about Griffin shutting her out without a call or text.

Maggie chewed a bite of her sandwich, studying Cassie closely. After she swallowed, she asked, "What now?"

Cassie shrugged. "That's up to Griffin."

C.J. squeezed her hand. "I agree, but it's obvious you love him."

Pain knifed through her. "I do, but I can't force him to change."

Her cousins nodded their agreement.

"What do you say to an afternoon spa treatment?" Maggie asked.

That was exactly what Cassie needed to get her mind off her problems. They paid for their lunch and headed for A Taste of the Irish that Maggie's sister-in-law owned. A bed-and-breakfast and tea house that also had a spa onsite.

Late that afternoon, the cousins hugged goodbye, promising to meet up the next day. Cassie went to the cabin for a nap before dinner.

Massive windows overlooked Lake Serenity as Cassie entered the main room. Grabbing a blanket from the sofa, she tossed it over her shoulders, then pushed open the sliding glass door. Snuggling into the deck chair, she watched the sun as it angled low in the sky. A flock of geese honked as they dropped down onto the glassy water. An otter darted across the lake taking a wide berth around the flock.

Cassie sighed and relaxed into the chair. As much as she enjoyed the quiet time, she missed the boys and wished they were here. Not that long ago she'd envisioned bringing them here with Griffin, but that dream had died with all the others.

Her eyelids heavy, she snuggled deeper into the blanket, drifting between wakefulness and sleep as the last rays of sunlight washed over her.

~

CASSIE HAD JUST FINISHED her dinner that evening and ordered a second glass of wine, when a familiar voice asked, "Would you mind some company?"

Gasping at the sound of Griffin's voice, her gaze shot up to find him towering over her. "What are you doing here?" Suspicion blossomed. "Did Chet tell you I was here?" Her emotions warred between hope and despair—hope he'd come for her and despair that nothing had changed.

"No, he didn't."

"Then how did you know I was here?"

"The boys told me where you'd gone."

"And you came all the way out here instead of waiting until I got home?"

His voice dropped an octave. "What I have to say can't wait."

"What's left to say?"

He was silent a moment. "Will you at least hear me out?"

What could it hurt? She gestured to the chair next to her.

The waitress arrived with her wine, and Griffin ordered a beer. After the waitress left, he looked at her.

The apprehension in his eyes made her want to reach out to him, but she resisted. "So, tell what you came to say."

"You were right. It's hard for me to talk about the past." He paused a moment, then continued, his voice wavering slightly. "Losing Bobby tore me to shreds. I was barely holding it together when I moved back to Hope's Crossing, but you and the boys helped me through it."

She tried to keep the bitterness from her voice, but couldn't. "Until you hit a milestone and went dark."

The waitress returned with his beer. He took a sip, then continued. "I didn't expect the anniversary of Bobby's death to hit me so hard, especially since becoming involved with you had eased my pain. But it slammed me just like those first days after he died. I wanted to crawl into a dark cave and never come out. I pulled away from you and everyone I love."

"And you expect me to believe that won't happen again?"

He shifted beneath her steady gaze. "No, I can't promise that. It's part of my DNA to go into hiding when I'm hurting. But I swear that I will make every effort to change and share my feelings with you."

His response surprised her. She'd expected assurances that he'd never shut her out again. Instead, he'd offered her the unvarnished truth, and she did the same in return.

"You hurt me—deeply, but not only me. The boys were lost without you, and I'm scared that the next time something triggers memories of Bobby or some other emotional trauma, you'll disappear."

"I know I'm asking you to take a risk with me, but I promise you I'll be there for you and the boys."

Cassie traced her finger over the rim of her glass before looking up at him. "I've never doubted that, but I feel like I'm always taking, and it makes me feel selfish."

Griffin's eyes turned bleak. "You asked why I couldn't wait for you to come home. Here's the real reason. I'm only half a man without you. I can't eat, can't sleep. I function on autopilot when you're not beside me. It's not life, it's survival. You think I do all the giving, but the truth is, you're the one who pulled me out of the darkness. You kept me sane and gave me a reason to get up in the morning. When you hold me, I can survive anything—even losing my son. It terrifies me how much I need you."

She touched his cheek, and he leaned into her hand.

His voice reverberated into her. "I love you, Cassie. I don't want to lose you. You are the woman of my dreams. I've been afraid to love again, but if you give me a second chance, I'll prove I'm worthy of you. Please don't give up on me, Cass."

Cassie drew him into her arms, and he melted into her. "I've missed you," she said.

"I've missed you more."

Cassie whispered into his ear. "I have a whole house within walking distance of here. What would you say to going there and spending some quality time together?"

He pulled back. "Really?"

She nodded.

The brilliance of his smile blinded her. "Show me the way home, honey."

～

THREE WEEKS LATER, Cassie rolled over and cuddled against Griffin. After they returned from Paradise Falls, she'd asked him to move in permanently with her and the boys, and he'd done so without hesitation.

Griffin's arm tightened around her. "Good morning." His voice rumbled in her ear still raspy with sleep.

Her favorite time of day—early morning before the boys woke up, warm and snug in bed with Griffin. "We slept in."

Griffin raised his head and glanced at the clock. "Seven o'clock, that's amazing."

Cassie nodded. "It is. I'm surprised the boys haven't been in here already. They've been so excited about Thanksgiving and all the food Aunt Luella and Dad are preparing."

Griffin nuzzled her neck. "I think next year we should have it here. Your aunt and Chet deserve a break."

"I tried to convince them we could have it here this year, but they wouldn't hear of it."

"Next year we'll both work on them."

Cassie liked the sound of that—that they would be together next Thanksgiving and many more after that.

"What do you say we have an early holiday celebration of our own?" Griffin asked.

Cassie rolled so that they were nose-to-nose. "I don't think I've ever celebrated turkey day in quite that way."

He kissed her, and a whole new kind of warmth spread through her. Before they went any further, the rumble of footsteps sounded outside their door.

"There may be a few disadvantages to sleeping in," Griffin murmured, a smile crossing his face.

Cassie concurred and appreciated a man who understood the impact having three children had on their love life.

She cupped his face. "Maybe we can escape later and find some time to have that special celebration."

He drew her hand to his lips and kissed her fingers as the door burst open. The boys tumbled onto the bed, shouting, "Happy Thanksgiving!"

Contentment filled her. Life didn't get any better than this.

THE NEXT MORNING AFTER BREAKFAST, everyone got dressed and went outside, the boys each clutching a balloon. They'd written a card to their father and tied it to the balloon. Cassie made one for her mom and Griffin had done the same for Bobby. Now they were going to release the balloons, sending their messages out into the Universe.

"Do you think it'll really get to Daddy?" Jeff asked.

Cassie looped an arm over his shoulder. "I believe he hears everything you tell him."

Trevor's scowl held the skepticism of a boy becoming a man. "There's no way he'll ever get these balloons."

"Why do you think that?" Griffin asked.

"It's just like Santa Claus," Trevor said.

Jeff's face scrunched with concern. "What about Santa Claus?"

Griffin gave Trevor an imperceptible shake of his head, then said to Jeff, "You've got to believe in Santa Claus just like you've got to believe these balloons and our messages will get to your dad and Bobby and Cassie's mom."

Jeff's eyes shone with absolute belief. "I believe."

Griffin drew Trevor off to the side and spoke softly to him. "You don't have to believe, but don't destroy your brother's innocent wonder. You're old enough to understand there is no Santa Claus. And maybe these messages won't go directly to the people we love, but the idea is to let go of our pain and loss through these messages. I think you can understand it from that perspective. This is hard, and you're hurting inside just like I am. But this is an opportunity for us to ease our pain. Do you understand what I'm saying?"

Trevor nodded.

Griffin drew him into his arms and held him close, whispering in his ear. "I know you miss your dad and you're hiding it behind anger. I miss Bobby, too, and I hide it behind guilt. We need to find a way to grieve and tell ourselves it's okay to miss them."

Trevor fisted his hands into Griffin's shirt. "I don't miss him. He left us. I hate him."

"Is it possible you can hate that he left you but still love him?"

Trevor raised tear-stained eyes and shrugged.

Griffin hugged him tighter then released him.

Trevor swiped the tears from his cheeks and went inside.

Cassie came up beside him, and Griffin draped an arm over her shoulder. "He's still struggling," he said.

Cassie leaned into him. "I think more so than the other two. He's older. He remembers more than they do."

"He does. I hope doing this will help, but if it doesn't, we'll find something that does."

He wasn't giving up. Trevor needed to see that he wasn't alone.

Cassie raised up on tiptoe and kissed him, then said, "Together we will find a way to help him."

"We will."

GRIFFIN'S PHONE rang as he finished the chart he was working on. He'd come to the office early Sunday morning after Thanksgiving to catch up on work while everyone was sleeping.

He saw the call was from Trevor and answered it.

"You have to come home now." The phone went dead.

Griffin dialed Trevor back, and it went to voicemail. He grabbed his coat and headed out the door. The charts would wait. Trevor needed him, and that's all that mattered.

He drove to the house and raced inside. "Trevor?"

A shout came down the hall. "I'm in my bedroom."

Griffin went straight to Trevor's room. "What's wrong?"

Trevor waved him over and pointed to the opened package on the bed. "Cassie found packages for everyone on the porch. It's supposed to look like it's from dad." Resentment oozed from each word he spoke. "I know you sent it."

Griffin looked at the worn baseball glove, a card beside it. "I didn't send this."

"You're lying."

Griffin gave him a long look. "Have I ever lied to you?"

Trevor ducked his head, muttering, "No."

"Well, I'm not starting now." He paused a moment to allow his words to sink in. "What does the card say?"

Trevor handed it to him, and he opened it.

I miss you buddy. I know Cassie and Griffin will take good care of you. Thanks for the balloon. Here's a little something to remember me by.

Love,

Dad.

Griffin laid it on the bed. "I don't know what to say. I didn't write this and neither did Cassie if that's what you're thinking. That is *not* her handwriting."

"Then someone else sent it."

Griffin sat down on the bed beside him. "Obviously, but there's nothing wrong with believing it was from your dad. He could've arranged for someone to send these after he died, or maybe someone found the balloon and sent this to you to make you feel better. Does it really matter? The question is, does it help?"

Trevor studied the glove, lifting it to his nose and inhaling, then gave a slow nod. "Dad and I used to play catch together, and this is the glove I used. It was just me and him."

"So, it gives you a good memory."

Trevor smiled, cradling the glove to his chest. "It does."

"Then that's all that matters."

Griffin didn't know who sent the gift, but he wished he'd thought of it. He squeezed Trevor's shoulder. "You okay now?"

Trevor nodded.

He left him and went into the bedroom he shared with Cassie. He found a package on his dresser addressed to him. Staring at it, he wasn't sure he wanted to know what was inside. Finally, he tore it open and stared at the cleats Bobby wore in the photograph in his office. He opened the card.

I miss you Daddy, but don't worry about me. I'm okay.

Love,

Bobby.

Griffin carefully laid the card back down, struggling to control the emotions overwhelming him.

Cassie's soft body pressed against his side, and her arm wrapped around his waist. "I didn't expect you home so soon."

He looked down at her. "I had a nine-one-one call from Trevor."

"About his package, I assume."

"Yes."

"What was it?"

"An old baseball glove."

"A sentimental gift like Jeff's stuffed animal Marie bought him, and Tyler's book that Raymond used to read to him before Marie died."

"What did you get?"

Moisture filled Cassie's eyes. "An original recording of the group Mom sang with when I was a baby."

Cassie ran a finger over the scuffed cleats. "These are adorable. I assume they have a special meaning for you."

Griffin swallowed back the urge to bury his emotions. "They do. I bought them for Bobby's first birthday, and he wore them everywhere."

Cassie's arm tightened around him. "A poignant memory?"

Griffin couldn't keep the huskiness from his voice. "Yes."

"Who in the world gathered all these things together?" Cassie mused.

Griffin stared at the gift. "My guess would be your aunt or your father, or both."

She sighed. "I wish I knew for certain so I could thank them."

Griffin considered her comment, then shook his head. "I like that the sender or senders didn't sign the cards. It follows the spirit of releasing the balloons, leaving a little mystery behind the gifts."

Cassie leaned her head against his shoulder. "I'm so glad you're here to share this with me."

Griffin pressed a kiss to her forehead. "Me, too."

Why had he ever gone it alone? Having Cassie to lean on made moments like this so much easier to bear. With the woman who completed him at his side, and he had everything he could ever need.

EPILOGUE

Griffin parked the truck in front of the Beauty Bowl two weeks later. A light snow fell as he followed the boys inside.

Stepping inside Sittin' Pretty, Griffin lounged against the doorway that looked out over the bowling lanes, watching as Cassie finished up for the day.

She looked up and smiled. "Griffin, what are you doing here?"

He crossed over to her. "The boys and I had some errands to run, and I thought you might need some help closing up."

"What kind of errands?"

He twirled a lock of her hair around his finger, ignoring her question. "Have I told you how much I love you?"

Her blue eyes sparkled. "Everyday."

His fingers tightened around the black velvet box in his pocket. He glanced out the glass wall to see three expectant faces pressed against the glass waiting for him to propose to Cassie.

Griffin faced her. Looking deep into her eyes, he dropped down on one knee. "Cass, I've arrived at that place where I can't imagine life without you. I love you more than anything in the world. Will you marry me?" He opened the box he'd picked up from the Wishing Stone, and the ring sparkled beneath the overhead lights.

With a trembling finger, Cassie traced the solitaire diamond ring. Her voice a husky a rasp, she said, "There is nothing I want more than to spend my life with you."

He rose and slipped the ring onto her finger.

"I love you, Cassie Cooper."

"I love you, Griffin Valentine."

Griffin gathered her into his arms and held up her hand so the boys could see the ring, then mouthed, "She said yes."

Shouts of joy echoed around them as the boys raced inside, jumping up and down and talking at once.

Without a doubt, Griffin had everything he needed. The one woman who understood him, and a ready-made family. He couldn't predict what the future held, but he was ready to embrace whatever life threw at him so long as he had Cassie at his side.

The end.

Preview
Forever Yours

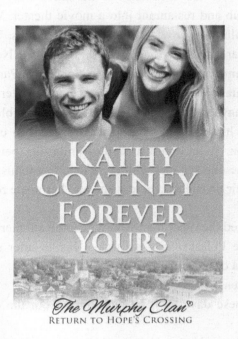

KATHY
COATNEY
FOREVER
YOURS

The Murphy Clan®
RETURN TO HOPE'S CROSSING

Paradise Falls, Idaho

Willa Dunbar sent the last of the staff home just after midnight to finish closing the theater herself. She liked this time of night. The quiet soothed her, made her forget all that was missing from her life.

She'd just finished cleaning when Charlie Pulaski's booming voice echoed through the theater as he called out her name. Her business partner, a barrel-chested bear of a man with a heart of gold, greeted her with his usual broad smile.

"How did it go tonight?"

"Excellent. We had a full house. I really think the Sunday night five-dollar special of popcorn and soda Jed suggested is drawing them in."

Charlie and his son, Jed, owned Pulaski's Bar and Grill. Three years ago they'd come to her with a business proposition. They'd wanted to convert the basement of the three-story Craftsman that housed their pub and restaurant into a movie theater. Willa would run the theater while they provided the food and drinks. She'd loved the idea, and a year later they had it up and running. Now she had her hands full running the pub movie house along with Paradise Fall's one and only Mountain View Drive-in—her original theater.

"He does have some good ideas," Charlie grumbled. Unquestionably, he loved his son, but Charlie was resistant to change, much to Jed's frustration. Willa didn't miss the similarities between their relationship and the one she had with her Uncle Cornelius, only those two worked out their problems whereas she and her uncle remained at odds each other.

Willa hugged the older man who'd become a father figure to her. In fact, the whole Pulaski crew had taken her in after she'd arrived in Paradise Falls a decade ago.

"Jed has plenty of good ideas."

"One of these days he'll be pushing me out the door and taking over."

Willa laughed. "Never. You two have the perfect arrangement. Jed runs the bar and the kitchen is your domain."

Charlie grunted and didn't disagree.

"So what are you really doing here, Charlie?"

"I can never get anything past you, can I?"

Willa grinned. "Nope, so spill."

Charlie blew out a weary breath and settled onto one of the sofas that filled the theater. Willa sat down beside him, waiting for him to continue.

"It's about Jed and Colleen. Their constant bickering is wearing on everyone."

Willa had noticed they'd been short with each other recently. "And?"

"And I was wondering if you'd talk to Jed. You've got a way with him none of the rest of us do, and maybe you can make him see he has feelings for Colleen."

Willa held up a hand. "Oh no. I am not butting into his love life." Besides which, with her track record, she was the last person who should be giving anyone relationship advice. She narrowed her gaze at Charlie. "You've already tried, and he told you to mind your own business, didn't he?"

Charlie toyed with the menu propped between the napkin dispenser and the basket of condiments on the side table. "He might have said something to that effect."

"So you're putting me in the middle."

Charlie's dark gaze met hers. "Maybe."

No maybe about it. That was exactly what he was doing. "I'll talk to him—" She shook a finger, "but whatever he tells me, stays with me."

Crestfallen, Charlie mumbled, "Okay."

Willa pressed a kiss to his cheek, then pushed to her feet. "I'm going home."

Charlie followed, sputtering, "What about Jed?"

"What about him?"

"You said you'd talk to him."

"I will, just not tonight."

"But—"

She squeezed his arm. "It will wait until I get some sleep. Tomorrow is soon enough, but I'm not a miracle worker."

She nudged him toward the exit. What she needed right now was a hot shower and bed.

#

Willa's phone rang, pulling her from a sound sleep. She fumbled for the light on the nightstand, knocking the cozy mystery about a dog, a human lie detector, and a cop onto the floor.

She swore as the phone rang again and answered it. "Hello."

A beat of silence, then, "Willa, it's Griffin."

She pushed up against the headboard, no longer groggy. Griffin, her childhood friend wouldn't call at two in the morning to talk. He was calling in a professional capacity as the local doctor. Her heart began to race.

"I'm sorry to call you so early," Griffin said.

"It's okay." Fear gripped her. "What's happened?"

"Cornelius had a heart attack."

Her fingers tightened around the phone. Uncle Cornelius still lived in her hometown of Hope's Crossing, and she'd had a close relationship him until she left Indiana and struck out on her own. Then he'd become *standoffish* as he would say, and whenever she went home to visit, there was always friction between them.

"Is he alive?"

"Yes, he is, and I'm hopeful he'll have a full recovery." He paused a moment, then continued. "I've tried to reach your sisters, but neither is answering."

They wouldn't. Hannah was in Scotland, and she'd spoken to her two days ago. A major storm was headed to the far north island where she was staying for the indefinite future. And Ellie was in the Australian Outback backpacking for three more weeks with no phone or internet.

"They're both out of country. Did Uncle Cornelius ask for me?" Willa's heart beat a little faster at the possibility that her uncle might actually ask for her over her sisters.

Another silence. "He's been in and out of consciousness since the ambulance brought him in."

Griffin was trying to spare her feelings. "He wanted Hannah and Ellie, didn't he?" she asked.

"You know how Cornelius is."

Stubborn as the day is long. "I do." Maybe this would be her chance to mend the rift between them.

"I-I appreciate the call, Griffin. I'll be on the first flight out."

"I'll let Cornelius know you're on the way."

The idea of seeing her strong, capable uncle in a hospital bed made her want to stay right where she was. But he needed her, so regardless of the strife between them, she would return to Hope's Crossing, take care of her uncle, and hopefully prove she

Order Forever Yours

Can't wait to read more of *The Murphy Clan*? Get Falling in Love… Again book one of *The Murphy Clan—Falling in Love* series, now!

ALSO BY KATHY COATNEY

Thank you for reading *Forever Mine,* the second book in the *Return to Hope's Crossing* series, part of *The Murphy Clan*. *The Murphy Clan* can be read as stand alone books, but there are also three series within the Clan— *Return to Hope's Crossing*, *Falling in Love*, and the *Crooked Halo Christmas Chronicles*. Book two, *Forever Yours*, Willa and Ben's story will be out March 2021.

If you liked this book, please leave a review. It is the best way to thank an author for a memorable read.

I love hearing from my fans. You can contact me through my website, newsletter, or join my Facebook group Kathy Coatney's The Beauty Bowl. I share information about my books, excerpts, and other fun information. If you like free books come join Kathy Coatney's Review Team by sending me an email kathy@kathycoatney.com.

All my books are small town, contemporary romances with uplifting stories of hope, a sprinkling of quirky characters and a happily ever after.

Contact me at:

Website

Kathy Coatney's The Beauty Bowl

The Murphy Clan

Return to Hope's Crossing series

Forever His

Forever Mine

Forever Yours

Falling in Love series

Falling For You…Again

Falling in Love With You

Falling in Love For The First Time

Crooked Halo Christmas Chronicles

Be My Santa Tonight

Her Christmas Wish

Under the Mistletoe

Crooked Halo Christmas Chronicles Boxset

Other Contemporary Romances

Leave Me Breathless

A Romantic Mystery

ABOUT THE AUTHOR

Kathy Coatney has spent long hours behind the lens of a camera, wading through cow manure, rice paddies and orchards over her thirty-year career as a photojournalist specializing in agriculture.

Kathy also loves—and writes—deeply emotional, small-town contemporary romance. Ironically, her books carry an agriculture thread in them, some more than others. Please note Kathy used to write these books under Kate Curran, but now writes all her books under Kathy Coatney.

Kathy also writes a series of nonfiction children's books, *From the Farm to the Table* and *Dad's Girls*.

CPSIA information can be obtained
at www.ICGtesting.com
Printed in the USA
LVHW091156151222
735287LV00008B/2371